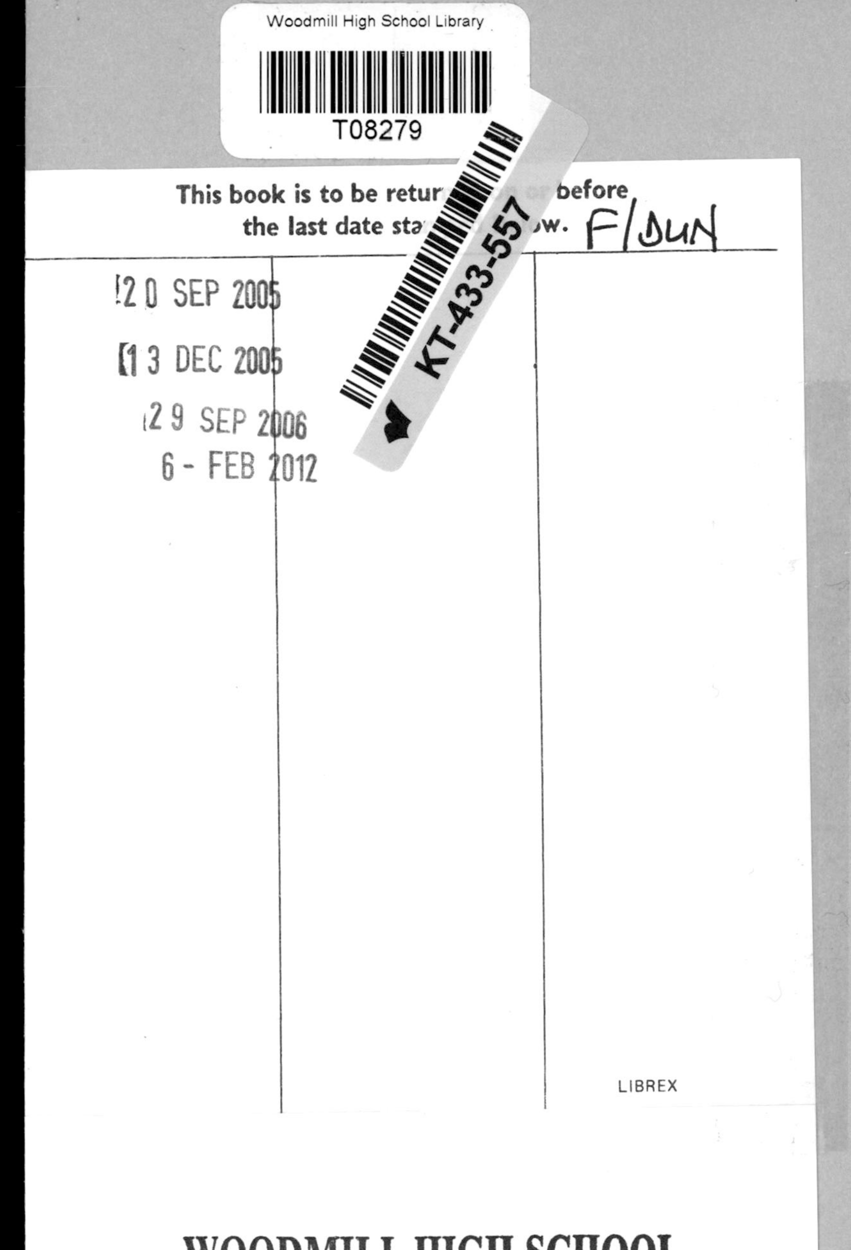

The Silver Bead

Look out for the other books in this trilogy:

The Lilac Tree
(previously published as *Zillah and Me*)

The Seal Cove
(previously published as *The Zillah Rebellion*)

Also by this author:
Snollygoster

Praise for Helen Dunmore's books:

The Lilac Tree

"well-written, funny and sad too"
Ella Fraser-Thoms, 12, Daily Telegraph

"two utterly believable child characters whose emotions leap off the page"
Daily Telegraph

"Dunmore is a wonderful storyteller"
Observer

Snollygoster

"Concise. Beautiful."
Daily Telegraph

"beautifully crafted"
Books for Keeps

The Silver Bead

HELEN DUNMORE

SCHOLASTIC
PRESS

Scholastic Children's Books,
Commonwealth House,
1-19 New Oxford Street,
London, WC1A 1NU, UK
a division of Scholastic Ltd
London ~ New York ~ Toronto ~ Sydney ~ Auckland
Mexico City ~ New Delhi ~ Hong Kong

First published by Scholastic Ltd, 2003

ISBN 0 439 98286 3

Typeset by Falcon Oast Typesetting
Printed and bound by Mackays of Chatham Ltd, Chatham, Kent

10 9 8 7 6 5 4 3 2 1

CHAPTER ONE

"School's out for ever!" yells Zillah, and she hurls her book-bag into the air.

"Zill! It's gone right over the hedge!"

"I'm only bothering to fetch it because I don't want our cows to get bellyache," says Zillah, as she lifts the loop of baling-twine and opens the gate.

"Aren't you sad about leaving?" I am. I can still feel the tightness in my stomach when we sang "One More Step Along the World I Go" at leaving assembly. I'm still sad, but Zillah doesn't care at all.

"I've been going on that old school bus for about a million years," she says. "And all the furniture in our classroom's too small. I've got bruises from trying to fit my legs under those tables. Everything's too small!"

Zillah whirls her book-bag above her head again.

"Mind out, Katie! I'm going to get it up on our barn roof!"

• • •

We're leaving. We're leaving. We're really leaving. We've been saying it so long that it's a shock to find it's not true any more. We're not leaving, we've left. Next year there'll be other kids sitting in our seats, or telling the little ones to get off the chestnut stump at playtime because that's where we sit. And Mr T won't be telling his jokes to us, or trying to teach us computer language so we can put stuff on our own website, or writing words in Russian or Greek or Arabic on the board so that we can understand that all alphabets work in different ways but they all do the same thing … COMMUNICATE! Mr T is crazy about communication, but it won't be us he'll be communicating with any more … and that seems strange to me, and a bit sad. The more I think of it the more the whole of primary school seems strange and far away and small…

• • •

It's the first morning of the holidays. Zillah and I are lying on her bedroom floor, surrounded by heaps of stuff which Zillah is throwing out.

"The worst thing is that my mum still treats me like a little kid," says Zillah. "And my dad thinks still thinks he's doing me a huge favour if he lets me drive the tractor. *There you are, girl, steady now, remember where your brake's to.* I've been driving that tractor since I was nine years old. I'm not going to roll it."

I've never driven a tractor, but Mum lets me drive our van up and down the lane from the farm to our cottage. I know how to change gear, and brake and steer and everything. Yes, I did scrape the wing once, but our van is so old and beaten-up that any new scrapes soon blend into the old ones.

Zillah and I have spent the whole morning sorting stuff into piles. Clothes that are too small, books with cartoons or pictures of cute animals on the front, and Zillah's amazing collection of sticker-books, are crammed into a jumble-sale binbag. Her school-books, millions of drawings, old diaries and all the rubbish from under her bed are in another binbag.

"Are you really going to throw your diaries away?"

"No. I'm going to burn them. When we've sorted out your stuff as well we'll have a huge bonfire."

"Um..."

I'm not sure I want to throw away quite as much as Zillah. I *like* old books I've had since I was about six, and maybe when I'm grown-up I'll want to look back at my school-books and...

"You have got one sock and two Barbie dolls without heads in your binbag," says Zillah two hours later, when we've finished doing my bedroom.

"Is it a white sock with a blue stripe down the side?"

"Yeah ... whitish..."

"I've been looking for that one! Give it here, Zill."

"You're down to two Barbies without heads, Katie."

"OK, they can go. Oh no, wait a minute! Zillah, remember that man in the Friday market who sells vintage Sindies and Barbies for about fifteen pounds each? Maybe he'll give me lots of money for these."

"I've never seen any headless Barbies on his stall," says Zillah, snatching the binbag from me. "Katie, your bedroom doesn't look any different."

"It's tidier."

"But is it emptier? Don't you want to change things, now we're going to secondary school?"

"Of course I do," I lie. "Zillah, you know those sticker-books you're throwing away? If you really don't want them..."

"You do."

"Mmm ... maybe..."

"OK. If you agree to throw away your Blue Peter poster."

"Blue Peter poster? I haven't got a Blue Peter—"

"And you're not having my stickers either. We're *secondary*-school students now, Katie. *Old.*"

"Zill, it's half-past two. Quick, we've got to help your mum set up the tables."

"Don't think you're going to make me forget about that bonfire, Katie."

But we are really late, and so we have to run up the lane and there's no time to talk about throwing things away or changing things or secondary school any more. Which is good, because I hate talking about it.

Zillah's mum, Janice, does cream teas for visitors up at the farm. Zillah and I are waitresses, and we also lay the tables, wash up and do the accounts, while Janice makes the tea, whips cream, and bakes batch after batch of scones and cakes. All the jam is home-made, too. We get paid two pounds an hour, and we get tips. Sometimes we get tips in foreign coins, which is annoying when the people who leave them are English. Sometimes we get twenty pence, or fifty, or even a pound if it's a big group and we smile loads. (I have had to give Zillah some training in this, as she is usually prefers scowling at strangers to smiling at them.) Zillah and I split all our tips.

• • •

It's a busy afternoon.

"They had two lots of cream, Zillah, did you put both on the bill?"

"What do you think?"

Zillah is brilliant at maths. She adds up like a streak of lightning, and she keeps trying to make Janice charge more for the huge, delicious cakes she bakes.

"You'll never make a profit if you don't even charge enough to cover your ingredients, Mum!"

"Well, Zillah, our hens laid the eggs which I used in the cakes. I didn't have to pay for them."

"Then you should charge even more, Mum! Free-range, home-made, organic, no chemicals. Let's put that on our sign!"

Five minutes later a camping van turns into the lane. Mother, father, grandma and two teenage children. Five cream teas, two walnut and coffee sponges and three strawberry tarts. And they bought one of Janice's chocolate cakes and left us a two-pound tip, and said they'd tell their friends to come here.

Janice sweats in the kitchen, warming up tray after tray of the scones she'd made that morning, filling teapots and making sandwiches for a family who decide they might as well have a proper meal while they're here. People have started buying whole cakes to take away, as well as the slices they eat here, because Janice's cakes are so good. I keep telling her she ought to have her own TV cookery programme. She is wonderful to watch in her kitchen, because she is so quick and sure and not clumsy at all. It's quite strange, because Janice is often clumsy outside the kitchen, with people as well as with things.

But maybe Janice wouldn't really make a TV star – not in her white pinny with red polka dots on it, and the frown that makes her look cross even when she's enjoying herself. If Janice was a waitress, I don't think she'd get that many tips.

We're going to make loads of money helping Janice with the cream teas every day, all summer.

The last customers finish their cream teas and drive away. I pick a fat red strawberry out of the bowl and eat it while the late-afternoon sun pours down, warming my back. The moment is as perfect as the strawberry.

• • •

It's the twenty-fifth of July and we've finished school and we're never going back. At least, not until September, when we start at secondary school in our new uniforms, all scared and not knowing where anything is and –

We were the oldest ones at primary school, but at secondary we'll be the little ones again. We won't know what to do or where to go, who are the nice teachers and who are the horrible ones. Or who the bullies are. But I'm not going to think about that now. It's six weeks away – nearly seven. That's like for ever.

It's the beginning of the school holidays and life is wonderful. As long as Zillah keeps forgetting about that bonfire, and I can sneak my Barbies back into the cupboard. I might find a couple of spare heads somewhere…

I don't play with them. I design clothes for them. I might be going to be a clothes designer, or maybe an interior decorator. I know what I want things to look like, and Mum says that's the most important thing. You've got to have vision.

CHAPTER TWO

They arrived this morning.

• • •

I'm in my bedroom now. The mist has come in suddenly and there's white woolliness over everything and glistening wet. I can't see anything but all the sounds are magnified. Zillah's dad's cows are joining in with the foghorn, and Mum's got her radio on while she works in her studio.

It was clear this morning. I was up at Zillah's place, painting the new sign (about the free-range eggs and organic jam) when we heard the engine. It came labouring up the road, then it slowed down.

"Someone for the caravan park," said Zillah. "I'd better go and see, Mum's gone over to Eglos Farm to borrow jam-pots."

At the top of the lane there's a gate into the field where Zillah's parents run their caravan park. It's just a field, with portable toilets and rubbish bins and everything. There's a sign telling people to call at the farm first, before they drive in. But when we got to the farm gate, a girl had already unlatched the gate to the caravan field, and she was swinging it open. Zillah frowned.

"You got to book your pitch at the farm first," she said. "And pay."

The girl looked us up and down.

"My mum said to open the gate and she'd drive into the field," she said. "Can't leave a van the size of ours blocking the road."

"You can pull in on the verge," said Zillah. "That's what people do."

"Your place, is it then?" asked the girl, as if she was laughing at Zillah.

"It's my mum and dad's farm."

But the gate was swung right back by now and the engine revved.

It was the biggest van that had ever come into the field. It skimmed the gateposts on both sides, but the girl's mum took it steady and got it in without a scratch. She was a big, frowning woman with two strong arms on the wheel.

It was not a normal cream-and-chrome holiday caravan. It was rusty orange, and it looked as if it had once been a small furniture van. There were windows cut into the metal sides, with bright flapping curtains. Strapped on top of the van was what looked like a sofa, wrapped in plastic. The van doors at the back were open, and a little red-haired boy was hanging off the metal bars. Inside, the van was bursting with stuff and people. Zillah and I stared at each other. Zillah said something to me but I couldn't hear over the noise of the van.

The woman backed her van into a big space by the granite hedge, near the stream. She'd picked the best pitch on the field. The engine raced and roared as it backed, then suddenly it stopped, the van lurched, and was still. Birds sang. Two campers who were on their honeymoon pulled back their tent-flaps and stared out.

People began getting out of the van. The little red-haired kid jumped off first, then a man holding a baby. He didn't look like the girl's father – he was much too young. He reached back into the van and fetched out another baby and then tucked them one under each arm, like puppies. Twins.

The last person out of the van was a crunched-up old woman who looked as if she was everyone's great-grandma. The girl helped her carefully down the step. Her face was brown and dry and wrinkly, and her eyes were the colour of the damsons on the tree by our cottage. She looked much too old to be bumping around the countryside in the back of a van. But maybe she liked it. She was the only one who looked happy. She gazed around and her damson eyes took in everything – the field, the honeymoon couple, the bright, fresh stream with ferns and flowers growing by it, and Zillah, and me. She hobbled over to the stream, sat down on a stone, pulled off her shoes and stuck her feet into the running water. I knew how it felt. I've paddled in the stream loads of times on my way back from school, after a long day and a hot ride on the bus. The water's icy cold and it tickles and prickles like fizzy lemonade.

"Are they twins?" I asked the girl.

"What do you think?"

"Boys or girls?"

"One of each."

"Wow."

"Five months old," said the girl. I couldn't tell if she was pleased or not. Her face was expressionless.

"I'm Katie, and this is Zillah."

"I got to help my mum now."

Quick and neat, the girl unfastened the straps on top of the van. The man gave one baby to the little rusty-haired kid, and the other to the old woman, then he helped the girl lift down the sofa. Carefully, they unwrapped the plastic. Underneath, the sofa was blue velvet. They brushed it clean, carried it over to a soft patch of grass by the stream, and set it down.

"You rest now, Great-Gran," said the girl. "I'll make your tea."

"Good girl yourself," said her great-gran, settling her bones into the soft blue sofa, closing her eyes, letting the sun warm her.

"You're all right now, Great-Gran," said the girl.

Slowly, Zillah and I moved away. It didn't feel like Janice and Geoff's caravan park any more. It felt like someone else's home.

• • •

There are huge arguments going on in Zillah's house. Geoff wants to move the van people off the farm right away.

"They're trouble," he said. "I know their sort.

Travellers. They won't pay us a penny and they'll squat here the whole summer, driving decent people away."

"She gave me fifty pounds," said Janice. "For the first fortnight. They don't how long they're staying yet."

"We charge five pound a night for a van that size. It ought rightly to be seventy pounds, for two weeks. And how do you know we'll see any more of their money, once the two weeks are up?"

"We haven't got anyone else wanting that space," Janice pointed out. "Fifty pounds is better than nothing."

"They'll be hanging their washing all over the campsite, making fires and leaving rubbish, letting their dog get at the stock—"

"They haven't got a dog," said Zillah.

"You sure of that? Dogs out of control I won't have on my land."

"There's no dog," said Janice.

"You sound as if you want them here."

"It's not what I'd have chosen. But she's got twin babies with her, and she paid her fifty pounds up front."

Geoff wasn't happy.

"You don't know what you're starting, letting travellers stay on the farm. I don't know what our neighbours'll say. What if there's another vanload of them coming up our lane tomorrow? You don't know what you're starting, having them here. Mind, if they make any trouble—"

"I can't turn off a woman with two babies who's paid me fifty pounds," said Janice, beating furiously at the chocolate-cake mixture for tomorrow's teas.

I backed out of the kitchen. The mist was coming up, rolling off the sea the way it does when hot air meets cold, deep water, far out. The foghorn began to boom.

• • •

I've been lying on my bed, thinking about it all. I wonder how long they'll stay? The girl is the same age as us. I wonder what her name is. I wonder if she lives in that van all the time. Maybe she doesn't go to school at all. Geoff says they're travellers. Where are they travelling?

I'd better make some food. Mum's been working for hours and I don't think she had any breakfast. If she doesn't eat she smokes too much. Mum thinks I don't know how much she's smoking, because she only smokes in the studio. Parents can be unbelievably stupid sometimes. She thinks if she opens the window wide and fans the smoke out, I won't smell it.

I'll make spaghetti with tomato sauce and meatballs. And I'll ask Mum what kind of travellers they are. Geoff looked so angry. But they paid their money.

"I won't have travellers on my land."

But if they're travellers, they'll travel on. They won't stay here. So what is Geoff worried about?

CHAPTER THREE

The girl's name is Rose. We heard her great-gran calling her, and the little red-haired boy is called Titus. I think he's her brother. I want to talk to Rose, but Zillah doesn't.

Rose came up to the farmhouse for eggs when Zillah and I were putting out tablecloths this afternoon. She didn't say anything, just knocked on the kitchen door for the eggs. Some campers pay for all their milk and eggs at the end of their holiday, but Rose paid straight away. I saw her slip a look towards us as she went by with her eggs.

I said hi, but she just sort of nodded.

"Friendly," said Zillah.

"She's all right."

"How do you know?"

"She's really nice to her great-gran. She's always bringing her cups of tea on that sofa."

The caravan park is taking on a different look. There's Great-Gran's blue velvet sofa set by the stream. At night they wrap it up in plastic in case it rains. There's Great-Gran's card-table, and Great-Gran's footstool, which has a blue velvet cushion to match the sofa, and Great-Gran's blue box with red roses painted all over it. I wonder what she keeps in that box. It has a lock with a key that Great-Gran hangs on a chain round her neck.

There's all the washing, but it's hung up on a line between the van and the hawthorn bush. I think it looks all right. Anyway, people have got to wash their clothes and dry them.

There are the engine parts of the van spread out on a tarpaulin on the grass. The carburettor needs cleaning, the man who isn't Rose's dad says. But it's Rose's mum who does all the work on the engine. I've seen her. I don't know the man's name yet, or Rose's mum's name.

They did light a fire the first night, but Geoff came storming up and now they use a camping-gas stove like everyone else.

"One of the holiday people complained to Dad," said Zillah. "About those engine parts laid out on the grass. She said it was dangerous, with children playing round."

"What did your dad say?"

"He said he'd speak to them."

"Your dad wants them off his land."

"Yeah, he does," said Zillah. She pushed back her tangle of hair. Her face was hard and thoughtful.

"You think he's wrong, don't you, Katie?"

"They're not hurting anyone. They're paying for everything. Rose paid for those eggs as soon as she took them."

"I know," said Zillah. She frowns. "Lift the other end of that table, Katie, it's wonky."

We carried on setting the tables. Zillah was deep inside herself, thinking.

• • •

Janice called me into the kitchen after we'd finished the teas. She gave me my pay, then she gave me a brown envelope with money in it.

"Take that up to the caravan park for me, would you, Katie? Rose gave me a five-pound note for the eggs, and I hadn't got change earlier."

I thought Zillah would come with me, but she didn't. She was brushing burrs out of Bobby's coat.

"I'm going to bath him," she said, not really looking at me.

"OK. Umm – see you tomorrow then."

"Yeah, see you tomorrow."

I walked slowly up the lane. There were smells of cooking on the breeze. I tried to identify all the different meals the holiday people were having. Beefburgers, definitely, and sausages. Something that smelled spicy – maybe chilli? I could hear children shouting and laughing, and there was a summer smell of cut grass mixed with the cooking smells. Geoff must have been in mowing the pitches. The gate was open and there were two boys playing tennis with a ball that swung round on a pole. Titus, the little rusty-haired kid from the van, was watching as if he'd like to join in.

Rose's great-gran was sitting on her sofa by the stream, playing cards.

"Excuse me – is Rose around?"

"Rose? She's gone down to St Ives with the rest of them. She won't be back till dark."

"I've got some money for her. Her change from the eggs. Mrs Treliske at the farm sent it."

Great-Gran's eyes sparkled. "Lay it down on my table there."

Great-Gran's hand hovered over the brown envelope, and then the envelope vanished.

"Can you make a pot of tea?" Great-Gran asked.

I looked around. There was nobody else to do it. Titus wasn't old enough to boil a kettle.

"They're all working down the town," said Great-Gran. "Leah left me my flask, but I don't like it. Tea doesn't taste right from a flask."

She took the key from around her neck, bent down and fumbled in her blue wooden box painted with roses. "Here's my canister. Here's my tea. That's a rare tea, you can't buy it in the shops. Can you make a pot of tea? I'll tell you how. One spoonful for me, and a spoonful for the pot. Mind that you warm the pot. A cold pot kills the tea."

My hands reached out for the tea canister. I felt as if Great-Gran was magicking me to do what she wanted.

"Stove's under the van, back-end," said Great-Gran, and she gave me a box of matches.

I lit the camping-gas stove, boiled the water and made the tea. Gran didn't take milk or sugar, but she had a special cup of bone china with gold round the top and more roses swirling over it. It was so fine you could hold it up and see through it.

Great-Gran sipped the boiling tea.

"What's wrong with having a fire?" she asked me. "I

like a fire. You can't look into the heart of a stove, for it hasn't got one."

I was afraid she was going to make me build a fire, and then Geoff would kill me. Her eyes were shut in the pleasure of tea-drinking.

"The Queen of England could not drink better," she said.

Quietly, I began to edge away from the sofa.

"You still there then?"

"Yes—"

"Tell Titus I want him."

Titus was still standing by the tennis game with his thumb in his mouth. His eyes were big and soft with tiredness.

"Your great-gran wants you."

He took the thumb out of his mouth.

"She's not my great-gran. She's Rose's great-gran."

But he went over to her. As I crept away before she could ask me to do anything else, I heard her saying, "Go on in the van, Titus, and fetch me my blue blanket stitched with red. The dew's coming down."

• • •

10pm

I know what work Rose does. She goes with her mum and Jesse – that's the twins' dad, but he's not Rose's dad – and they do hair-wraps down by the harbour. Rose told me. And Titus isn't Rose's brother, he's Jesse's cousin, but Rose's family look after him.

I was throwing out the washing-up water on our vegetable patch half an hour ago when I heard someone running down the lane. I thought it was Zillah, but it was Rose.

"My great-gran says you made her tea."

"Yes—"

"She says you make better tea than me."

"She had to tell me how to make it. Mum and I only have tea-bags."

"She'd like that. She likes telling people what to do. What were you doing up at our van?"

"I brought your change, from the eggs."

"How much was it?"

"I don't know. Janice put it in an envelope."

"You gave it to Gran?"

"She said to put it on her table."

Rose shrugged. "Doesn't matter. We did all right down at the harbour today."

Her voice was bright with boasting.

"I get five pounds an afternoon for helping with the teas up at the farm. Plus tips," I said.

"They'd want to be big tips," said Rose.

"How much do you charge for hair-wraps?"

"Pound an inch. Your length of hair –" she measured my hair with her eyes – "that'd be be eight pounds."

"How long does it take to do it?"

"Your length of hair, twenty minutes with the beads and all."

Twenty-four pounds an hour. And it wasn't just Rose doing it – there was her mum, and Jesse. Someone would have to look after the babies – but still there'd be two people doing wraps for twenty-four pounds an hour for eight hours a day. That would be... Three hundred and eighty-four pounds a day. It can't be that much. It would only be that much if they were wrapping hair all the time without stopping. But even if it was only two hundred – or a hundred and fifty—

"It's an art," said Rose quickly. "We do patterns no one else knows."

"It's really expensive."

"I don't charge that much for people I know," said Rose.

"Don't you?"

"No. Only ninety-eight pence an inch if it's a friend."

I stared. Slowly, she winked. Her eyes were just like Great-Gran's.

"I could teach you," said Rose. "One day. Who lives here with you?"

"My mum."

"My dad went away too," said Rose. "He's up north."

"My dad didn't go away. He died."

As soon as I'd said it I wished I hadn't. It sounded as if I was saying, *Your dad chose to leave. Mine didn't.*

"Has your mum got a boyfriend?" asked Rose.

"No."

"My mum's got Jesse. She had the twins with Jesse."

"So he's your stepdad."

"He's twenty-one," said Rose. "That's only ten years older than me."

"Do you want some salad stuff?" I asked. "We've got

more than we can eat here. It all grows at once."

I pulled her two heads of lettuce, a bunch of spring onions, and radishes.

"My great-gran'll like those onions. She'll cut an onion up on a plate and sprinkle salt on it and eat it just like that. She says onions are good for her blood."

I shook off the soil and wrapped the salad stuff in newspaper. Rose took the parcel. It was getting dark, but just when I was wondering if she'd like to come in the cottage and maybe see my bedroom, she said goodbye and ran off up the lane.

"See you!" she shouted when she was out of sight. Her voice floated back through the duskiness that was beginning to thicken into night.

I think she does want to be friends.

CHAPTER FOUR

"If they earn that much, they'll have no trouble paying my dad for the pitch," says Zillah, when I tell her about Rose and the hair-wrapping down at the harbour. "Wonder how long they'll stay then."

"People do hair-wrapping down at the harbour the whole summer."

"I know. You reckon they'll stay the whole summer, Katie?"

"Don't you want them to?"

Zillah shrugged. "They've a right to be here, same as everyone else. But that's not what my dad thinks. He doesn't like travellers."

"Why not?"

"He's a farmer."

"Rose says—"

"You going to be friends with Rose, Katie?"

Zillah pushes back her hair and stares at me, fierce and challenging. It's as if the old Zillah's come back, the one I first met, before she was my friend. But why does she care so much if I make friends with Rose? It doesn't make any difference – it doesn't make me less Zillah's friend—

"Maybe you'd rather wrap hair with Rose than serve the teas up here," says Zillah. And it's back, the Zillah scowl I haven't seen for weeks and weeks. Months even.

"Great idea, Zill," I say. "Be back in a minute, I'm just going down to tell your mum I can't help here any more and she'll have to find another waitress from somewhere..."

Her eyes flash. For a second she believes me.

"You really think I'd treat your mum like that," I say. The flash goes out of Zillah's eyes.

"I wish they hadn't come here," she says. "Everything was all right before they came."

I remember what Zillah said, the day we cleared out her bedroom. *Don't you want to change things, Katie?* But I don't say anything.

"Listen, Zill, let's go down and see what they do. Let's go over to St Ives, and go round the harbour."

I really want to see Rose doing the hair-wrapping. I want to see her fingers flashing in and out, earning twenty-four pounds an hour. I'd like to see the babies, and Rose's mum, and even Jesse.

But Rose's mum is a bit alarming. She's not a cuddly, motherly person. She looks so strong, and she doesn't smile, and she knows how to sort out the inside of an engine. Meeting Rose and her family is like tasting a food you've never eaten before.

"All right," says Zillah.

"What?"

"I said all right. Let's go into St Ives. We can get the early bus on Monday."

Monday is our day off. It's the quietest day for teas, and Mum helps Janice then.

"Let's bring our swimming stuff."

• • •

Swimming-stuff, money, book (Zillah), pack of cards for a new trick I'm learning (me), bottle of water –

"Take the suncream," says Mum.

"Mum, I don't need it any more. Look how brown I am."

"Do you want to get skin cancer?"

"Do you want to get lung cancer, Mum?"

"Suncream, Katie. It's going to be hot today."

"Mum, how many cigarettes are you going to smoke today?"

"That's got nothing to do with it. I'm your mother. It's my job to make sure you don't get skin cancer."

"It has got something to do with it, Mum. I don't want you to die."

We stare at each other, shocked. The words just slipped out. They were words I meant, but I didn't mean to say them. If I don't watch out I'll say the next bit, the one I always think but never say. *I've only got you now. I can't lose you as well as Dad.*

"It's only ten a day, Katie. I'm trying to give up, you know I am."

Mum, I don't think you count them when you're busy painting. You just fumble for the pack without looking and put a cigarette in your mouth and I bet if I asked you, you wouldn't even know that you were smoking.

You would know the exact shade of green you were working into the blue of the sea, but you wouldn't know that there was a cigarette in your mouth.

But I don't say any of that now.

"Are you and Zillah taking your bodyboards?"

"No, we'll be walking around loads, so we don't want to carry them."

"Make sure you swim between the flags."

For heaven's sake. Zillah and I swim by ourselves down at the cove all the time. And we go out on our own in Zillah's boat, *Wayfarer*. We are really careful.

"Mum, we're going to Porthmeor Beach. There are lifeguards. We know what we're doing."

"I know, I know you're very sensible, Katie, it's just that I worry sometimes –"

I know, Mum. I worry too. About you.

"Mum, you won't forget to go up to the farm and help Janice at half-past two, will you?"

"I certainly won't," says Mum triumphantly. "I've set the alarm clock, look!"

Mum's big red alarm clock is balanced on a metal baking sheet.

"Why's the clock on there?"

"It makes more noise that way," explains Mum. "Listen."

She turns the clock hands round. There's a second of silence and then the alarm clock erupts. It jumps up from the baking sheet, crashes on its side and drums against the metal, ringing furiously.

"All right, all right, Mum! I believe you. You won't be able to work through that."

"I tried it while you were out," says Mum with satisfaction. "Maybe I could patent it."

"Mmm – maybe –"

CHAPTER FIVE

As soon as we get to Porthmeor we see how good the waves are, and wish we'd brought our bodyboards.

"We've got money," says Zillah. "Let's hire boards. And we can hire wetsuits as well."

"But Zillah, it costs loads."

"We're working every day, aren't we? What's money for if we never spend it?"

She's right. It's just that I have to be careful. I want to buy some new trainers, so I'm saving up my waitressing money. I can't ask Mum, because she's just paid the rent and the electricity bill. Her art materials cost so much, too. Paint and canvas are expensive, and Mum has to pay for framing as well. I wish Mum would sell another painting soon. She's got a huge canvas of Hellesveor Cliff on sale in Robert's gallery, but although lots of people come in to look at it and stand back and look again and ask the price, no one's bought it yet. It costs loads, I have to admit. Much more than Mum's ever charged for a painting before. But Robert says it's time she raised her prices. I hope he's right. Also, as Mum says, that painting is too big for most people's houses. It would look wonderful in the entrance hall of a huge glass building – you would feel as if you were walking into the dazzle of sun over the sea beyond the cliffs—

"Katie? Hello? Are we going surfing or not?"

We hire the boards. We hire the wetsuits too, because without them the Atlantic is too cold to let you surf as long as you want. Zillah and I aren't great surfers. It's too dangerous to surf on our part of the coast, and we don't come into St Ives that often. When I look at some of the kids who go to surf school every Saturday, I realize how not-great we really are.

But I love it, all of it. Paddling out to wait for a wave, letting the waves go if they've peaked too early, feeling the tension build when you see the wave coming, the right wave, the one that's going to lift you and sweep you in so fast it feels as if you're flying. And you don't think of anything else. All your worries vanish, and all you think of is now. This wave, the next wave, the next. The salt and sand up your nose when a waves crashes on top of you and wipes you out. The bruises you don't even notice until afterwards. The power of the water moving towards you, gathering force, beginning to rush but breaking just right so you catch it and you rush with it on the sweep into shore.

There are so many surfers out today. When we first got here we saw Mark and Bryony from school, but they're over in the malibu board area. They come to surf school regularly, and they've got their own boards and wetsuits and everything. Mark let us have a go on his board but we were even less great on that than we are on the bodyboards, so we watched him instead. He came in on the wave as it unzipped, his body crouched into the shape of the water's curve, riding with it, knowing where it was going and how to go with it. We shaded our eyes against the dazzle to watch him come in. Then he was off his board and waist-deep in water, grinning at us. He was just Mark again, not the surfer on the crest of his wave who could have been anyone.

The best moment comes one time when we've paddled our boards out and we're waiting for a wave. We are in a clear space of water, poised, feeling the swell hump beneath our boards. Bubbles fizz and glisten around the boards. We see the wave coming, a good one, and we paddle fast to get into position and then I feel the lift and just before it comes I look at Zillah and she looks back at me and her face is smiling wide and I know mine is too because I can feel it just as I can feel the speed of water gathering under me and starting to lift and rush me inshore.

"Wow," says Zillah. We've been swept in among the little kids, in less than a foot of water. We both look back to see how far the wave has carried us.

"Our hire time's nearly up."

"Just one more wave."

"OK. Just one more wave."

There's always one more wave. Not this one, not the next, but the one that's just forming, out at the horizon where the turquoise water darkens to a blue you don't get anywhere else but on Porthmeor. You don't need to think of anything. Because everything you want is here.

• • •

We have sausage and chips on the beach. The gulls circle us but they have no chance of grabbing any of our food. When I first came to live in Cornwall, I lost a 99, an almond slice and a cheese and tomato sandwich to the gulls, on three separate occasions. I'm more careful now. They dive-bomb you from behind, so that one minute you're holding a double-cone ice cream with a Flake stuck in it, and thinking luxuriously about which bit you'll eat first, the ice cream or the Flake, and the next you're holding the shell of an empty cone and watching a gull zoom back up into the sky with your ice cream inside it. Gulls have strange eyes when you look at them close-up. They are yellow, and hard, and they fix on you with no expression at all. When you look at them closely it's easy to believe that birds are related to dinosaurs. Imagine a gull seven metres long with giant claws, sailing through the air above you—

"More ketchup, Katie?"

• • •

We walked from Porthmeor down the Digey. All around the harbour was packed with people. It's so frustrating if you're trying to get anywhere in a hurry, because you have to pick a way between pushchairs and couples twined together and babies and families. Everyone's slow and they stop to look at everything, and then you nearly fall over them.

Zillah hates it. Normally she would never come round

to the harbour or Fore Street in high season, because people pressing all around her make her feel trapped. I suppose it's because she's lived all her life on the farm, on their own land which runs down to the sea. She prefers our cove where there's nobody else except the seals.

But I like it here. I suppose it's because I'm from London and so I like seeing all the different people and hearing all the different voices. On a wet day when everyone's circling round in waterproofs it makes me think of being on a bus in London in the rain, with more and more people pushing in. Mum used to lift me up on her knee so someone could sit down, when I was little, and I'd press my face against the window and feel the vibration as the bus hauled its way uphill. I used to feel so safe. Mum would say things like, "Dad'll be home early tonight, Katie. Maybe he'll take you to the park, if it clears up."

I thought things would never change. I'd always be going on big red buses, and hearing Dad ring on the doorbell because he'd forgotten his key for the thousandth time, and going up to the park with him on my pink bike.

But I'm hundreds of miles from London, and Mum sold my pink bike when I went into the Juniors, four years ago. It is one year and two months since Dad died.

• • •

A big family group stops just in front of us and we can't get past. They're trying to decide whether to take a boat trip to Seal Island. They are from London, I can tell from their voices. London voices are so different from Cornish voices. Suddenly a thought strikes me.

"Zill, how do I talk now?"

"?"

"I mean, do I still talk like I used to when I first came here? Do I still sound London, or do I sound Cornish?"

"You don't sound Cornish," says Zillah slowly. "But you don't talk as fast as you used to. When you first came I couldn't believe how fast you talked. You know when we make popcorn and the grains all start popping against the lid of the pan at once? The way you talked used to remind me of that."

How strange. Imagine Zillah thinking that, and not telling me. I thought the way I talked was perfectly normal.

"Don't slow down too much though, Katie," says Zillah. "You might get like my dad, thinking about everything for a million years before he opens his mouth. And then not much comes out."

"Zillah, you are so horrible about your dad."

"I'm not. I'm just truthful."

The London family stops arguing about who will get a reduced fare and who won't, and steps into the road without looking. A big Japanese four-wheel drive car brakes hard and the driver sticks his head out of the window and begins to shout abuse at one of the children. But the London dad isn't having that. He shoulders his way forward and leans down until his face is almost touching the driver's face.

"What's your problem, mate?"

People gather round. The driver stops shouting. The London dad is big, and the hand he is resting on the inside of the car window looks as if it could quickly turn into a fist.

"You want to watch your language," the London dad goes on. "This is a family resort, this is. Lucky for you I'm on my holidays, so I'm in a good mood. Now clear off out of here."

He takes his arm off the car window, and turns back to his family.

"All right. Who wants an ice cream?"

As the four-wheel drive slinks away, I see Rose. She is paying no attention to what's going on. A little girl is sitting on a stool in front of her, and Rose is working on her hair. There's an embroidered rug spread under the stool, by the harbour railings. On the rug there are big cushions, so people can relax while they wait their turn. On one cushion a baby twin is sleeping, but there's no sign of the other.

Rose frowns in concentration, and her fingers work fast. She's just as quick and skilled as I thought she would be. The little girl's hair is being wrapped with pink and orange and lilac and gold threads, and there are pink and orange beads waiting in a glass saucer. Already you can see the effect, like a sunset on a perfect evening.

Zillah and I drift closer. Rose's mum isn't there, but Jesse's busy wrapping another girl's hair. She's a teenager, with brown hair that must be about ten inches long. Ten pounds. The girl looks as if she likes Jesse, and I wonder if she's made the connection between him and the sleeping baby. You wouldn't immediately look at Jesse and think "Dad". He looks much too free and young. His teeth glint as he smiles at something the girl has said. But you can tell that Jesse isn't nearly as good at hair-wrapping as Rose. The colours he's chosen are much more ordinary, and he isn't wrapping as tightly as she was.

I notice that Rose has kept her own rainbow box of coloured threads down by her side, away from Jesse. He hasn't got nearly as many colours to work with as she has. I wonder suddenly if Rose likes Jesse.

As if Rose has heard me thinking about her, she looks up.

"Hi, Katie."

"Hi."

"You come to have your hair wrapped?"

I smile and shake my head.

"I spent my money on hiring a surfboard and wetsuit."

"You can still have it done. You can owe me if you want."

"No, I can't, I'm saving up—"

"There! Have a look at yourself, Tamsin," says Rose to the little girl. She holds up a mirror and moves it slowly from side to side. Tamsin is so pleased that her face turns pink as she looks at the rainbow patterns of the wrap, and her mum starts saying how great it looks and how she wishes she could have hers done as well. They pay out the money without seeming to care at all about how much it costs, and Rose gives them change from the leather bag around her waist. Then she smiles at the next customer.

She is so professional.

I can see the spools of thread in Rose's box more clearly now. They are beautiful. Rich, silky, glowing spools of colour. She has so many shades of every colour, and they are carefully arranged in order, from darkest to palest. The blues go from rich, dark midnight blue to the pale, translucent blue-white of ice. I come as close as I can to look at them, but I don't touch, because I've got the feeling Rose wouldn't like it.

"Where did you find so many colours?" I ask.

"I collect them. You can't buy these colours in shops."

She is so like her great-gran, saying how rare her tea was, and that you couldn't buy it in shops.

"Rose," Jesse calls across. "I'm out of pink. You got a pink there?"

Rose glances at him. Her hand goes down, but not into her box of colours. She reaches into a plastic bag that hangs on the railings and brings out a spool of pink thread. She tosses it across to him, and he catches it almost without looking.

"Cheers, Rosie."

She tenses. For a moment her face is so unfriendly that the customer gets worried.

"Isn't it all right if I have green with blue?"

Rose snaps back into her work.

"Course it is. Here, this green's got a bit of blue in it,

it'll shade into that dark blue you want."

Suddenly I realize that Zillah isn't watching. She's leaning forward, with her hands over her face.

"Zillah! Are you OK?"

"Dosebleed," comes Zillah's muffled voice through a wad of tissue. I fumble for more tissues in my backpack, and hand them to her. We shuffle over to the railings so she can rest against them, with her head in her hands.

It is a really bad nosebleed. Blood spreads right through the tissues.

"Keep your head still, Zillah."

Rose has noticed what's happening. Her eyes rest on us for a moment but her fingers don't stop wrapping, and her face is smooth as she chats and smiles with the customer. Zillah huddles with her knees drawn up to hide her face. She hates people seeing her when she's ill or upset. And there are so many people at the harbour, pushing past, their sandals and bare feet almost stepping on us. I put my arm around Zillah's shoulders.

"Is your friend all right?" A big sunburned woman bends down to us.

"She's got a nosebleed. Have you got any spare tissues, please?

More wads of tissues are handed down to us, and a plastic bag to put the used tissues in. The woman tells Zillah to pinch the bridge of her nose, then someone else stops and tells Zillah to put her head back. Their voices argue above our heads.

"No, she shouldn't do that. Pinching makes it worse."

"She ought to get her head forward, not back."

"My gran used to drop the back-door key down my back," chips in a third voice.

I move closer to Zillah. I am certainly not going to let anyone drop keys down her back, or push her head in any direction at all.

After a while the bleeding stops, and Zillah gets up slowly and cautiously.

"Let's go, Katie."

"Are you all right?"

"I'm OK. It's happened before, but this is the worst."

"Maybe it was all that surfing –"

"But I always dive loads, down at the cove."

I nod. It's true. Zillah is an amazing diver.

She still looks pale. Carefully, we pick our way through the crowd that has gathered around the hair-wrapping. Rose hasn't stopped work. This customer is almost finished (Rose has blended the threads so that the wrap has the colours of the sea in it, green and turquoise and deep, rich blue), and there's another girl waiting. Her curly brown hair must be eight inches long at least, maybe nine. Eight or nine more pounds to go into the leather bag fastened around Rose's waist. No wonder she didn't stop work to see how Zillah was.

"Come on, Zill. I've still got four pounds fifty left. Let's go and have hot chocolate, and then we'll get the bus home."

• • •

We sit in the café, the steam of our hot chocolate rising from the mugs on the table between us. Zillah still seems far away, lost in thoughts I don't share. At last she says abruptly,

"I don't like her, Katie."

"Who, Rose?"

"Yeah. She doesn't like me, either."

I think back. Has Rose ever tried to be friendly to Zillah? Maybe she thinks of Zillah as one of the Treliskes who want her and her family off their land. She doesn't think of her as someone who might be a friend.

"Why don't you like her, Zill?"

Zillah shrugs.

"I don't have to have a reason, do I? I just don't like her, Katie. I wish she hadn't come here."

I want to say to Zillah that she's being like her dad, judging Rose and her family without getting to know them. But I don't say anything. Zillah looks so pale, and I'm worried that the bouncing of the bus will make her nose bleed again. I just want to get us home.

CHAPTER SIX

Mum is watering the tomatoes when I get back. She waves, shading her eyes against the evening sun, and suddenly I realize what has changed.

Mum looks happy.

"Did you have a good day, Katie?"

"It was all right. Zillah –"

But I stop myself. I'm not going to tell Mum about Zillah not wanting Rose here, and Rose wanting to be my friend but not Zillah's.

"What about Zillah?"

"She had a nosebleed."

To my surprise, Mum looks thoughtful.

"She's been looking peaky. And Janice said she had a temperature the other night. Maybe you two should have more than one afternoon off each week."

"We can't do that! We need the money."

"If there's anything you need, Katie, you can ask me for it," says Mum, flushing.

OK, Mum, I'd like a mobile … a new computer in my bedroom would be good, too, especially now I'm going to secondary school and I'll have lots of homework … and they've got a top I like in the surf shop opposite Woolworth's…

"It's just I'm saving up for something," I say aloud.

Mum doesn't ask any more questions. Maybe she thinks I'm saving up for her birthday in September. I feel mean, knowing that what I am really saving for are my new trainers, though of course I'll get Mum a good present, too.

"You should make the most of the summer," says Mum, drowning a tomato plant. "Time enough to work and worry about money when you're older."

Isn't it weird how even someone who is quite perceptive, like Mum, imagines that being young means you have no worries? Or wants to imagine it. In my opinion, the worries you have when you're young are much worse than adult worries. If an adult doesn't like her job, she finds a different job. If a child doesn't like her school, that's too bad. Her parents and teachers have little talks about it, but nothing changes. If an adult gets bullied at work, it's called harassment and the person who does it goes to court. Bullying at school is just normal. The most worrying thing about being a child is the way things happen without you even knowing about them, let alone choosing them. *Oh, by the way, Dad's got a new job. We'll be moving to Stoke-on-Trent. You'll lose your friends, your school, your home. But don't look so worried! You'll soon settle in. Adults are the ones who have the worries in life. Not children!*

Mum's not like that. She tells me about things. In fact sometimes I have to remind her to be a bit more worried.

"Have you opened those bills you hid behind the

clock yet, Mum?"

"They weren't urgent," says Mum firmly. "I've paid all the urgent ones. You shouldn't even be thinking about bills at your age, Katie!"

I stare at her. Mum knows perfectly well that I always open all our bills, because Mum hates brown envelopes and so she hides them away without opening them, and then she can't always find them. This has led to problems in the past, so now we have a system where we put away money every week in a jar for electricity and coal and wood for the stove. Mum puts all the child benefit in there, and she gives me money to buy phone stamps from the post office every week, to save for the phone bill. (We haven't had the phone long, and I'm determined we're not going to get cut off. If you have ever had to live without a phone, you will know what I mean. I am never, ever going to have to wait outside the village call-box in the rain again, waiting for someone to finish a conversation that goes on until all the glass of the call-box is steamed up with their breath. In fact, after I've bought the trainers, I'm going to start saving for a mobile.)

When we get the red reminder bills, Mum and I open up the jar and sort out the money and so far there's always been enough to pay them. It's good system. However, it's clear that Mum is on Planet Parental Responsibility this afternoon.

"It's my job to sort out our finances."

"But you do, Mum. You earn all our money. I only help you a bit with sorting out the bills."

"Oh dear. Don't tell anyone at school, Katie."

"Of course I won't."

I give Mum a hug. "I think the way we live is good."

"Mm. I wouldn't mind having an inside toilet. Another winter of walking down that path in the rain . . . Katie, you would tell me, wouldn't you, if you were embarrassed about it? I mean, when your new friends from secondary school come round?"

"Mum, it's fine! Nobody from school cares. They like it here because they can do whatever they want."

"Oh dear," says Mum again. "I hope they don't tell their parents that."

• • •

After Mum has gone inside, I take a stroll down to the outside toilet, and look at it hard. Will my new friends from secondary school laugh at it? No one from primary did.

I like it, anyway. It's whitewashed outside, like a little house. It has a corrugated-iron roof, and in winter the rain hammers down as if someone is playing piano on the roof. The toilet always smells of Jeyes Fluid, because Mum cleans it every day. She doesn't bother much about the rest of the house, as long as the kitchen and toilet are clean. The walls are white, and usually there's a spider or two quietly making its web in the ceiling corner. I don't mind that any more, although I used to be terrified of spiders. There so many things I'm not terrified of any more, since I came to live in Cornwall:

1) The dark. There is so much dark around here that you just have to get used to it. And once you are used to it, you begin to notice that it's hardly ever really dark. The stars are so much brighter than city stars, and the moon shines so strongly that I can walk down from Zillah's house to our cottage by moonlight without ever switching on my torch.
2) Walking alone down country lanes. Sometimes a cow moos suddenly and makes me jump, but down here there aren't lots of drunk people or people on drugs. I know nearly everyone who goes by, and they always say hello.
3) Being alone in the cottage. I don't mind it at all now. If it feels a bit too quiet I open the door and listen to the noise of the sea.
4) Something happening to Mum. I used to think about this all the time at first, after Dad died. I still do sometimes, but it doesn't make my heart pound and my hands shaky any more.

And loads more things. Spiders, and crossing fields with cows in them which might be bulls, and swimming in very deep water, and getting caught in a rip, and having to talk about my project work in front of the class.

No, I'm not frightened of any of them now. I'm still frightened of some things – but it's better not to write them down. It makes them grow larger in my mind if I think of them.

"Katie! Katie!" It's Mum, calling from the cottage door. "Your friend Rose is here!"

CHAPTER SEVEN

Rose is holding her rectangular glittery box with the handle.

"I'm going to wrap your hair," she says, as soon as she sees me.

"But – Rose, I told you, I'm saving for trainers."

"I'm doing it for free, Katie, cos you're my friend."

I must have stared at her a bit too long because she adds sharply, "Aren't you?"

"Yes, of course –"

I take her inside our cottage. She looks around with the same bright sharp look, taking in everything. The bowl of deep-purple plums in Mum's favourite yellow dish, the jar of marigolds on the table and the big pot of marguerites on the deep window ledge. Mum's sketches of Hellesveor Cliff taped on the wall. While she's working on a painting she usually tapes sketches up in here as well as in the studio, so she can keep seeing them and getting ideas from them. She'll take these down soon, once she starts another painting.

"Did your mum do those?"

"Yes."

"Can you draw like that?"

"No." I say it firmly, because I don't want Rose asking to see my sketchbooks. I've got one sketchbook for clothes design and another for interiors. Zillah looks at them sometimes.

"That's a pity," says Rose. "You could do portraits at the harbour. There's a girl down there who does them, but she's not as good as your mum."

"It's a different kind of drawing," I say. "People want portraits that look like photographs." (I'm not going to tell Rose, but I did once suggest to Mum that she could do portraits like that, one day when we'd had a lot of red bills all at once. But Mum explained to me that it was a different kind of drawing.)

"D'you think your mum would give me one of her drawings?" asks Rose.

"I don't know."

Rose puts her glittery box on the table and opens it. There are her rainbow spools of thread, her beads, and the cardboard rings she uses to pull the skein of hair through to be wrapped.

"Let's have a look at my colours," says Rose. She gives me a close, assessing look, then her hand hovers over the spools. "I think we'll go for yellow, cos you've got a tan, and with dark hair like yours it'll look good."

She takes out a bright, pale sunny yellow, then a richer buttercup.

"And we want something darker to go with it. Trust me, it'll look good."

She picks a spool of thread which is the colour of clear honey, and some amber beads.

"You sit on that stool."

Rose takes longer than she took with the paying customers at the harbour. After ten minutes or so Mum comes in, goes through the kitchen to her studio, then comes back again with a box of pencils and a block of paper. I don't think Rose notices. She's frowning, concentrating on the pattern of colours she is creating.

"I've got to do it tight, because your hair's slippy," she explains.

Mum sits down quietly in a dark corner of the kitchen, and begins to sketch. None of us speaks for a while, and the room is full of Mum and Rose's concentration.

"Nearly done," says Rose at last. "I'll finish it off with the beads."

I don't want to look until she's finished

"Go and look in the mirror," says Rose.

I cross to the mirror that hangs over the clock. It is beautiful. Honey and buttercup and pale sunshiny yellow, all beautifully wrapped around my hair. Something glitters between the two amber beads Rose has used on the end of the wrap. It looks like silver. A long silver bead, with patterns on it.

"That's my lucky bead," says Rose.

I lift the bead up to the light. The pattern on it looks like tiny writing, but there aren't any words I can read.

"You can keep it," says Rose.

Mum has finished her sketch, and she comes over to look at the wrap.

"Those colours are beautiful," she says. "They've got real depth."

"I collect them," says Rose, and I hear the pride in her voice. I think of the cheap, sugary pink thread she threw to Jesse. No, she certainly doesn't like him.

"I sketched you while you were doing Katie's hair," says Mum. "Have a look."

Rose takes Mum's drawing. She frowns, and I'm worried in case she's angry at the way Mum has drawn her. Then she says, "Can I have it?"

"Yes," says Mum, " but let me pull the page out. It might tear."

The drawing isn't like a photograph, but it is like Rose. It shows the fierceness of concentration in Rose's face, and the skill in her hands. She looks powerful.

"It's good," says Rose. "My great-gran'll like it."

She smiles as she carefully rolls up Mum's sketch, and then Mum disappears to find a rubber band to put round it.

"It's the best hair-wrap I've ever seen," I say, fingering the cool silver bead. I wish I was on my own so I could look really close in the mirror. I don't know Rose that well, and she might think I'm vain if I stare at myself. But it's the wrap I want to look at, not myself. It's like a sunburst of colour, and the silver bead make it even more brilliant.

"Your friend Zillah'll be wanting one," says Rose, and I fall straight into her trap.

"Will you do Zillah as well?"

"Course I will. If she pays me two pounds an inch. Farmers have got plenty of money."

It would be no use trying to explain to Rose about

Zillah's parents. She wouldn't understand how hard they've had to struggle to try to keep the farm going. I don't think she'd care either. If only I could make her understand how it really is. If only she could see Geoff up on the barn roof in the pouring wind and rain, trying to patch it with heavy-duty plastic. The plastic flapping in his face, and Janice gripping the bottom of the ladder, in case the wind blows it down. If only she could see Janice, up at five every morning, her face creased with worry when her hens won't lay.

"They're not rich, Rose, things have been bad for them, there's been BSE and then foot-and-mouth and—"

"Farmers are always moaning," says Rose coldly. "They don't care about us so why should we care about them?"

I open my mouth to argue, and then Mum comes back into the kitchen, so I don't say any more. But the hair-wrap doesn't look quite as beautiful now.

I'll never tell Zillah what Rose said about charging her two pounds an inch, but Zillah is going to see my hair-wrap and she's going to know that Rose wants to be friends with me, and not with her. Suddenly a horrible thought strikes me. Is that why Rose did it? So that the hair-wrap would be a sign of her friendship, separating me off from Zillah?

No, it can't be that. Rose is smiling at me.

"You look good, Katie," she says. "Come up and show my great-gran some time. She likes you."

CHAPTER EIGHT

There is so much trouble at the farm.

Jesse's brother Nathaniel arrived with four friends in another van yesterday morning. Zillah and I saw it all because we were adding FRESH RASPBERRIES TODAY to the sign for teas up at the top of the farm lane, and then the van turned in. Geoff wouldn't let them stay. Jesse's brother shoved a handful of ten-pound notes under Geoff's nose and told him that his was as good as anyone else's money and then Geoff really lost his temper and went off and got his shotgun, and then Jesse's brother asked if Geoff was threatening him, and Geoff said no, only going shooting vermin.

Nathaniel's friends all got out of the van and stood around Geoff and Nathaniel. Then Leah (Rose's mum) came charging out of their van with the babies and shouting, "Leave it, Nath! You're going to blow this one for all of us."

After that Nathaniel and his friends got back in the van and drove off, blaring their horn and yelling abuse out of the windows so that all the holiday people who weren't already watching what was going on (like it was a film) came out of their tents and caravans and started asking Geoff what was happening. By this time Janice had come running up from the farm and Leah talked to her for ages and in the end Geoff calmed down and let Jesse and Leah and Rose and all of them stay. For now.

Rose didn't do anything. She just sat on the blue velvet sofa with her gran and watched. When she saw me watching her, she winked, a big slow wink as if we had a joke together.

Zillah says her dad would never have used his shotgun on Nathaniel. He brought it out to show them that he'd got it. Geoff says he's going to get another dog, a proper guard-dog, because Bobby is too soft.

Rose didn't look as if she cared at all about what happened to Nathaniel, or his friends, or Jesse, or any of them. She watched it all as if she was watching TV.

• • •

But the next thing that happened was worse. We went down to the farmhouse after Nathaniel and his friends had gone off in their van. Janice was upset and Geoff sat on the end of a stone trough and started polishing the butt of his shotgun and suddenly Zillah had another nosebleed, much worse this time than the one she'd had at the harbour. Blood was splashing down into the yard dust. It was horrible. Even Janice was worried, you could see.

"Maybe we should take her down to the doctor," she said, hovering over Zillah with a pile of tissues. But Zillah wouldn't go.

"Id's odly a dosebleed," she kept saying.

But it was the worst nosebleed I've ever seen. At last the bleeding stopped and Janice made Zillah sit very still so she wouldn't start it up again. Then Zillah said she wanted to go and lie down in her bedroom.

"You come up too, Katie."

"You ought to rest properly," fussed Janice. "I'll get you a hot-water bottle and a paracetamol."

"I want Katie to come," said Zillah, and so we all trailed upstairs and Zillah lay down on her bed and Janice started organizing duvets and hot-water bottles and hot drinks and windows a bit open until I could see that Zillah was ready to scream. Janice can't help it, but she is one of these people who are noisy even when they're trying to be quiet. And then Janice started giving instructions, as if we were both about three years old.

"Why don't you look at your stickers with Katie, Zillah, and then maybe you could both do some nice quiet reading – or a game of Scrabble—"

"Mum. Please. I'm OK. It was just a nosebleed."

Janice flushed and looked hurt. She loves looking after people, but unfortunately Zillah is no good at being looked after. Janice straightened Zillah's duvet one more time and then looked at us both in a hopeful sort of way.

"I'll bring the Scrabble up, Zillah."

Zillah buried her head under the duvet. Janice likes us playing Scrabble because she thinks it is educational. Zillah and I completely hate it. Once Janice was out of the room Zillah heaved a deep sigh.

"See what I mean? She's stuck in a time warp."

"She's only trying to be nice."

"She's trying to be nice to someone who isn't me," said Zillah fiercely. She sat up.

"Do you feel awful?" I asked cautiously.

"No. I'm just tired."

She looked awful. I thought maybe I should go, but Zillah said, "Don't, Katie. Did Rose do your hair like that?"

"Yes."

"How much was it?"

I hesitated. But I wasn't going to lie to Zillah.

"She didn't charge me anything. My mum gave her a drawing."

Zillah sighed again. "She likes you. And she doesn't like me."

"I don't think it's because of you. It's because you're part of the farm, Zill."

"Do you like Rose, Katie?"

I hesitated again, but this time it was because I really didn't know. Did I really like Rose, or was I just flattered because she wanted to be my friend? I thought of Rose's quick fingers doing the hair-wraps, and her sudden smile, and her damson eyes which were exactly like her great-gran's, and the way she sat on that blue velvet sofa in the middle of a field and didn't seem to care that she had no permanent home, and the way she didn't go to school and was independent and had her own money –

But then I thought of the way Rose watched Geoff and Nathaniel and Jesse arguing as if it was TV, even when Geoff got his shotgun out. She didn't look frightened or worried. In fact she looked rather … satisfied … and the way she winked at me, as if it was all a joke…

I wasn't sure that I could rely on Rose – but there was something fascinating about her –

"I've never met anyone like her before," I said slowly.

"I wish Mrs T was back," said Zillah, surprisingly.

But Mrs T and Mr T and all the little Ts were on holiday with Mrs T's mother in London. I could just imagine the little Ts rioting around the Zoo and the Science Museum and the tops of double-decker buses, leaving a trail of wild excitement, crisps and soggy biscuits everywhere they went. London wouldn't know what had hit it. Our computer-crazy, science-loving Mr T would be in his element. Natural History Museum, Museum of Childhood, London Eye…

I felt a touch of homesickness for London at the thought of it all. I could just see Mrs T tearing down the Old Brompton Road with the baby bouncing in his buggy and the little ones running alongside. Mrs T is only twenty-five, much younger than Mum or Janice.

Zillah talks to Mrs T quite a lot. She tells her things she can't tell her mum.

"They'll be back next week," I said. "Is something the matter, Zill?"

"No," said Zillah, but her eyes were dark with thought. Then she said, "Let me have a look at your hair-wrap, Katie."

I showed her, and Zillah touched the silver bead.

"It looks like writing – but it's not writing –"

"Rose said it was her lucky bead."

"It looks old," said Zillah dreamily. "Maybe it's a bead

from Abyssinia, or a bead from Babylon. I wonder where Rose got it?"

"She collects them. She's got this beautiful box, it's full of different threads and beads."

But Zillah had lost interest. "What's that noise, Katie?"

I went over to the window and looked down. Janice was dragging chairs and tables into place on the terrace.

"Oh my God, Zillah, I forgot the teas. Your mum's doing all the work. Quick, I've got to go."

Zillah pulled back her duvet and swung her legs over the side of the bed.

"Don't be stupid, Zillah. Your mum's not going to let you work today."

And I could see that Zillah was quite glad to lie back again and snuggle under the duvet, even though it was a sunny day.

"We'll still share the tips," I said.

"You don't have to, Katie."

"It's OK. I'll smile loads and give them extra clotted cream. The tips'll be huge."

At the door I paused and looked back to say goodbye, but Zillah had already closed her eyes.

CHAPTER NINE

Rose's mum has nearly finished mending the van's engine. Geoff is pleased about this, because he thinks that they'll leave once the van is fixed, but Rose told me yesterday that Jesse and Leah want to stay all summer.

"We're making good money in St Ives. It's better than Newquay this year," Rose says.

Rose has been telling me about how she lives. In the winter they stay in one place for three or four months, and sometimes Rose goes to school. But I don't think she goes often. She doesn't like school. Thirty kids and one adult stuck into one room seems crazy to her. And having to put your hand up and ask when you want to go to the toilet makes her laugh. Rose says she can learn things when she needs to learn them.

People laugh at you in schools if you don't know the same things they know, but Rose knows different things. A girl called Marijke taught her hair-wrapping over in Newlyn, two summers ago. She gave Rose some of her best threads to start Rose's collection, and gave her the glittery box. Rose says she lived in Marijke's tent all that summer.

Rose's life is so free. I think Leah would let her do

anything she wanted. But Rose says Leah takes most of Rose's hair-wrapping money, to keep them all in the winter. And her great-gran wants Rose's money, too.

"My gran's the worst. She's always after what I earn."

Yesterday Rose gave her great-gran a twenty-pound note. Her great-gran smoothed it out and held it up to the light to check it, then she tucked it away in her bag.

"She's got hundreds in there," said Rose. "She gets us to buy her tobacco and humbugs, so she doesn't have to spend her money."

But she didn't say it as if she minded. Rose's great-gran is like the queen of their camp, even though she never does anything but sit on her sofa, drink tea, smoke roll-ups she rolls herself, and suck stripy mint humbugs. Rose says that her great-gran had ten children when she was young, which may be why she doesn't get too excited when Titus throw lumps of mud at the van or tries to spit all the way across the stream.

I think Titus wants someone to play with. The other holiday people won't let their kids play with him.

Great-Gran tucks up her feet on the sofa and sits and dreams while the blue smoke from her roll-ups wreaths around her head.

"How old is she?" I asked, but Rose didn't know.

"She says she's as old as her tongue and a little bit older than her teeth."

Rose is the one who earns most money. Jesse works for a while then he goes off to the pub. Leah is mostly busy with mending the van, cooking and taking care of the little ones. The babies roll round on their rug while

Titus plays (spits and throws mud) and Leah replaces part of the van's exhaust. If the babies roll off towards the stream, Gran lets out a squawk and Leah rolls them back again. Rose doesn't help with the babies, although she'll make sandwiches for Titus, and take him down to the farm with her to get the milk and eggs. But she won't look after the babies, and Leah doesn't make her.

"They're hers," Rose says. "Hers and Jesse's. No one asked her to have them."

I'm not sure I would want as much freedom as Rose has.

Rose says she knows what the writing on my silver bead means. It says "Your life will be fortunate". I asked her how she knew but she just shrugged.

"Somebody told me," she said.

I wonder if my life really will be fortunate. I think it will. When I'm down at the cove, lying on the warm sand at low tide, feeling the heat of the sun on my back, listening to the waves and the cry of the gulls, I know it will.

• • •

Zillah and I are going down to the cove soon. Zill's feeling better today, and she's promised her mum she won't dive in case it starts another nosebleed. Janice has forced us to have two days off a week, which is bad for buying my trainers but wonderful on a day like this when it's so hot that clotted cream melts into little yellow beads. Zillah's bringing some of Janice's gingerbread, which has a sticky topping with whole almonds stuck into it. She'll be here in a minute.

• • •

It's six o'clock. Everything still feels strange, as if the world has turned upside down and then back again, and I'm dizzy from it.

Zillah and I have always fed the seals. We were sunbathing on the rocks this afternoon when we saw their heads bobbing in the glitter by the mouth of the cove. We weren't even going to swim until I saw them, because Zillah was tired. The seals come in for mackerel when we're fishing, and often they come in for company.

Seals look like dogs when they're in the water, swimming alongside you. Like black retrievers, or labradors, with whiskers and big dark eyes that always look as if they're laughing at something. But when they dive they don't look like dogs at all. They are as sleek and powerful as the waves.

"There they are, Zill! Let's swim out to them!"

I was ahead of Zillah because she wasn't swimming as fast as usual. The seals saw us coming and dived. Sometimes they do that so they can go deep under the water then come up right beside us. It's a game they play, and it's a bit sudden but great when you get used to it. When they go down, you always think they've gone for good, because they can hold their breath so much longer than we can.

Suddenly they were up beside us, so close we could touch them. Two sleek heads, two powerful sets of shoulders, glistening with water. Seals are big when you're up close to them. And they're strong.

Then it happened. The big seal closest to Zillah was suddenly too close. All at once he was much bigger than her, and much more powerful. I was so close to him I saw the water standing off in drops from his thick coat, then there was a swoosh and the other seal knocked me aside and under the water. I came up and he swooshed past me again, not touching me this time but sending a wave into my face.

I coughed, and spat out a mouthful of sea. The big seal was face to face with Zillah. His head was higher than hers and it looked as if he was trying to put his flippers on her shoulders. Zillah kicked backwards, but the seal followed her. It pushed and her head vanished in a froth of bubbles. She came up, coughing and pushing at the seal with her hands. But the seal was too strong for her and he wanted to go on playing. Zillah's head went down again in a swirl of water.

"Zill!"

And it was over as suddenly as it had begun. The seal rolled over lazily, as if it was bored, and shook his whiskers. He dived, and this time he came up twenty metres away. The other seal was bobbing at his side.

Zillah coughed, treading water.

"Are you all right, Zillah? What happened?"

"He was playing. I'm OK."

Her mouth was set tight.

"They're coming back!" A flash of panic went over me as the seals dived. I held my breath. There was so much deep water around us, black in the shadow of the rocks. The seals could come up anywhere. They could get between us and the rocks and we wouldn't be able to climb out –

But they weren't coming back. It was just a game, and now it was over. We saw them, heads sleek in the dazzle of light, heading out of the cove to the open sea. In a few seconds they were gone. Slowly, we swam to shore and hauled ourselves up on to the rocks. As Zillah clambered out, I saw a streak of red on her shoulder.

"He scratched you!"

"I know." She peered at her shoulder. "I felt it. But it's all right, Katie, it's nothing."

"I never thought the seals would hurt us."

"He didn't mean to. He was playing." Zillah squeezed water out of her hair. "The water's his place, not ours. He thinks we can do everything he does."

"But they've never played like that before."

"It's only a scratch. My dad told me once his grandad had his finger bitten to the bone by a seal."

"You never told me that."

"I only just remembered it," said Zillah.

I shivered. Out in the water, all at once, everything had changed. I'd seen how powerful the seals were. Strong enough to drown you. Not because they wanted to hurt us, but because the sea was their element and it wasn't ours.

"You won't tell anyone, will you, Katie? Mum'll stop me swimming here."

"No, I won't tell."

"The seal didn't mean to hurt us," Zillah said again. I saw that it was important for her to believe that. Zillah's cautious with people, but not with animals and the sea and wild places. Nothing's going to change that.

"I think I'll go and see Granny Carne," said Zillah thoughtfully.

Granny Carne is the exact opposite of Rose's great-gran. It's impossible to imagine her spending the day on a blue velvet sofa. Granny Carne strides for miles over the downs and along the cliff tops. She can scramble the most difficult paths down to the coves, and she'll go right out on the rocks at low tide to pick mussels. But of course she's young, compared to Rose's great-gran. Granny Carne isn't anyone's granny, although everyone calls her that. She has no children, and she lives alone in a grey granite cottage high on the Downs, and she can tell your fortune if you go to see her. She's tall and strong, like a protecting tree.

"Do you want me to come with you?" I asked. Zillah frowned, thinking. I didn't mind, because that's one of the things I like about Zillah. She is so honest. She never pretends to want to do things if she doesn't.

"Not this time, Katie. I'll go on my own," she said at last. I like Zillah being honest, but all the same I felt a pang of hurt.

How stupid can you get, Katie? Just because Zillah is your best friend it doesn't mean she has to take you everywhere she goes, like a teddy bear.

I wonder what Zillah wants to find out from Granny Carne? But I am definitely not going to ask.

CHAPTER TEN

"Katie?"

"Yes?"

"You sound funny."

"– in the garden – ran for the phone –"

It's lucky I'm out of breath. I still feel strange about Zillah not wanting me to go with her to Granny Carne's, and what I feel comes out in my voice even when I don't want it to.

"Listen – Katie –"

Now it's Zillah who doesn't sound like herself.

"Katie – you know this morning?"

"Yes."

"Well, are you doing anything?"

Am I doing anything? Sewing all the name tapes on the new school uniform Mum and I bought in Truro at the weekend. Helping Mum clean the windows because we both agreed last night that it was stupid to live in a cottage with amazing views over the fields to the cliffs and the sea if you could never see those views because the windows were always dirty. Hacking down the nettles which are now a serious health hazard on midnight trips down the garden...

"No, I'm not doing anything special. Not until I come up to your place to do the teas."

"Would you – I mean, do you want to come up to Granny Carne's with me?"

"OK," I say. It's quite tempting to say more, such as *Why do you want me now, when you didn't yesterday?* or *Are you sure you wouldn't prefer a private chat with Granny Carne?* But for some reason I don't.

"Thanks, Katie," says Zillah. And she does sound thankful, and somehow a bit shaky, too. Not like Zillah at all.

• • •

The sun is hot as we climb the path to Granny Carne's. I don't think I've ever seen so many butterflies. Painted ladies, red admirals, cabbage whites, and clouds of small brown butterflies with yellow-tipped wings. I don't know what these are called. They flutter on yarrow and clover, and settle on clumps of nettles under the hedges. We stop loads of times to look at them. Zillah is tired, because it's so hot.

I love the greyness of the stones round Granny Carne's. There are the standing stones, the loggans, and her cottage is built from the same grey granite, and the walls around it are granite too, waist deep in bracken and montbretia. The cottage looks as if it's grown out of the hill and one day it'll grow back into it. There are purple foxgloves, and clumps of rosemary and lavender.

It's a very still place, and in the stillness the

buzzing of the bees is loud. You can imagine all the history that has happened here, people getting born and people dying, and wars far away, and ships being wrecked on the sharp black rocks that run out under the sea. And all the time the bees gathered nectar and pollen, and Granny Carne's cottage stayed the same, with its back against the hill and the sound of water trickling from the spring into Granny Carne's stone trough. Sometimes I wonder if she's been here all the time, through all that history. No one seems to remember when she was born. They say she's always been here.

Granny Carne is waiting for us. This is something I've given up trying to understand. We never tell Granny Carne that we're coming – no one does. But she is always expecting you. She has laid teacups and some of Janice's gingerbread on the table. We recognize it at once.

"Has my mum been up here?" Zillah asks.

"She came a day or two since," says Granny Carne.

Zillah scowls. I know exactly what she is thinking. *Granny Carne belongs to me, not Mum. What's she doing up here?*

"What was she doing up here? She never comes to see you."

"Same as you I daresay," says Granny Carne mildly.

I try to think what Janice might have wanted to ask Granny Carne. Maybe something about the farm, or money. Janice is always, always worrying about money.

"Have some gingerbread," says Granny Carne.

"I'm sick of gingerbread. Our house is like a

cake-shop," says Zillah. "All my mum wants to do is stuff people with food all day long."

"Maybe Katie'd like some."

I take some gingerbread, and pour a glass of spring water from the jug. Granny Carne's water is cold and pure on the hottest day. She doesn't have piped water, or gas or electricity, or a telephone. She cooks her food on a stove, has open fires, candles and lanterns. But Granny Carne doesn't waste candles. She goes to bed with the sun and gets up with the sun. Long days in summer, short days in winter.

I eat my gingerbread while Zillah drums her fingers on the table, looking pale and cross. But I refuse to feel guilty about taking a second piece. Cake may be more common than cornflakes in Zillah's house, but it isn't in mine. Zillah is probably thinking of Janice back at the farm, engaged in another cake-baking marathon. Some days just the thought of Janice is enough to make Zillah fizz and prickle.

"So you wanted to ask me something," says Granny Carne to Zillah.

Zillah stops drumming her fingers. She lays her hands flat on the table and stares at them.

"Yes. But I don't know – Katie, you tell."

I swallow a whole almond in surprise. "Me? What –"

"You know, about the seals. Tell Granny Carne what happened with the seals when we were swimming," says Zillah, as if we've talked about it beforehand.

"Well, the seals –" I begin, then I stop. I feel so nervous, even though there are only Zillah and Granny

Carne in the room. I feel as if the seals are listening too, judging what I say, deciding whether they'll let me back into their friendship or not.

"Well, we were in the water – swimming down at the cove..."

Granny Carne listens with her eyes on my face, drawing the right words out of me. I want to explain how sudden it was, and how the seals changed from being our friends to being wild and powerful creatures who might do anything, in their own element. And that the sea was their element, not ours, no matter how much we swam in it or sailed *Wayfarer* on it. When I've finished speaking, Granny Carne is silent for a while. She seems to be waiting for more.

This time it's Zillah who speaks.

"I want to know what it all means," she says. Granny Carne nods thoughtfully.

"Yes, you're ready for knowing that," she says. "It means changes, Zillah. Your life's going to go in another direction, not the one you know. You've got to face up to it now. You'll need a fighting spirit where you're going. That's what the seals have showed you."

"What do you mean – where am I going? I can't leave here. This is my place. I can't live anywhere else."

"Katie had to leave her place," says Granny Carne. "She was at home in London and then she came here and now she's at home here. You can do more than you think you can, Zillah. You'll leave, and you'll come back, and you'll be strong, just like the seals showed you how to be. You won't let anything push you down."

"I'm not going anywhere!" shouts Zillah. "They can't make me! I'm not leaving. Is this something else my mum and dad are planning without telling me?"

Zillah's face blazes with anger. She looks like Zillah again, not quiet and pale but fierce and crackling with life.

Granny Carne nodded approvingly. "You keep that spirit in you, Zillah."

The angry light dies out of Zillah's face. She looks confused now instead of furious. "When the seal pushed me down," says Zillah slowly, "it was hard to come up again."

"Did the water draw you?" asks Granny Carne, and I don't know what she means, but Zillah does.

"I was looking at the inside of the waves, with bubbles coming up through them, and I thought I belonged there, down inside the water. Not up on land."

"But you kicked out, Zillah!" I say. Something in what she says frightens me.

"Yes, I did," says Zillah, frowning and trying to remember. "I must have. I got scared, and I fought back up, and then the seals went."

Granny Carne has been listening intently.

"You kicked out because you wanted your life, Zillah," she says. "That's what you want to remember.

"I'm tired," says Zillah in a puzzled voice. "I don't know why it is. I'm always tired now. I can't row *Wayfarer* because I get out of breath."

So that's why we haven't been out in *Wayfarer*. Not because of the weather, or the leak that needed fixing, or the other reasons Zillah gave me.

"I'm not a magician. I can't tell you anything you don't already know, inside yourself," says Granny Carne. Then she reaches out, takes Zillah's hands, and holds them in her own hands for a moment. The blaze has gone right out of Zillah's face and she is pale again. Granny Carne isn't stern now, she's gentle.

"You grow more like your great-aunt Zillah every year," she says. "She never liked gingerbread either. Your great-aunt Zillah was the best friend I ever had."

In all the centuries you've been here, I think to myself, and I smile, but my eyes prickle as well. A storm of thoughts blows in my head. Why does Granny Carne want Zillah to be a fighter? And why does she talk about Zillah leaving? Zillah can't leave, she belongs here, she doesn't want to go anywhere. And why didn't I notice that Zillah couldn't row *Wayfarer*? When was the last time we went out in *Wayfarer* together?

The stillness and peace of the day has gone, and when we leave the cottage I'm surprised that the garden is peaceful, the butterflies are flirting their wings on the lavender bush, and the bees are bumbling in and out of the foxgloves, as if nothing has changed at all.

• • •

Zillah can't leave. It's impossible. I wish Granny Carne would say things clearly, instead of in riddles. But Zillah seems to like what Granny Carne meant. She looks much more cheerful on the way home, and she doesn't snap at Janice once the whole afternoon, even though it is boiling hot and we have about a million irritating customers who can't make up their minds what they want.

"I'll have raspberry jam with my scones. No, strawberry. Or did you say the raspberry's home-made? Maybe I'll try that then. Oooh, look, Philippa, they're having strawberry over there, it looks delicious, doesn't it! But the raspberry's organic. Oh dear, it's so hard to choose. Could we be a terrible nuisance and try them both?"

You certainly could be a terrible nuisance, I think grimly, but I'm not going to let you.

"One pot of strawberry, one pot of raspberry," I say firmly, and they smile as if I've sorted out their future for them. Just like Granny Carne.

• • •

It's late, but the phone still keeps ringing. Mum's had loads of calls this evening, about the exhibition she might be having at the Centennial Gallery. It would be so fantastic if it happened that Mum is in a frenzy of excitement and keeps tripping over things on her way to grab the phone. This will be another call for her so I'm not going to answer it.

"Mu-um! Phone!"

I hear Mum downstairs, crashing open the studio door and immediately falling over the pile of laundry that I haven't got round to putting in the bathroom cupboard yet.

"!!!! *****! KATIE! Are these your clothes on the floor?"

"No, Mum, they're YOUR CLEAN DUVET COVER

AND SHEETS," I yell back with satisfaction. The phone rings and rings until Mum disentangles herself from the sheets, grabs the receiver and barks out YES? HELLO? in a voice which would surely scare off any potential painting-buyers or exhibition-organizers.

Sometimes it's inconvenient that the ceilings in our cottage seem to be made of cardboard and that you can hear every word through them. At other times it's useful.

"Oh! Janice!" says Mum, in a voice of total surprise, as if the last person she would ever expect to hear from is her best-friend-from-childhood who lives just up the lane and whom we see or speak to at least once a day.

It's only Janice, so nothing interesting there. I wind the duvet round my head so I don't have to listen to every word, and then I remember that I hid half a Crunchie from myself in the back of my bedside cupboard. And it's still there. Slowly, luxuriously, I begin to nibble off the chocolate all round the sticky golden centre … and downstairs Mum's voice goes up and down, up and down, but much more quietly now so that I can't hear the words. Not that I would want to anyway … not if it's only Mum and Janice.

I start thinking about Rose and whether she would teach me to do hair-wrapping, and then I could do amazing wraps on people at my new school. I am deep in thoughts of colour combinations and beads when I realize that the Crunchie wrapper is empty and that downstairs it is completely silent. Mum's not on the phone any more, but she hasn't gone back into the studio either. The cottage sounds completely empty and silent, as if it's holding its breath.

I raise my head from the duvet and listen. Still nothing.

"Mum?"

More silence. Then Mum's voice, sounding much further away than just downstairs with a thin ceiling between us.

"Yes, Katie?"

"Was that Janice on the phone?"

"Yes."

I don't know why, but when I hear the way she says "yes" I'm off the bed and across the bedroom, through the door and down the stairs. Mum is sitting at the kitchen table with the phone beside her. She looks up.

"Watch out, Katie, you'll fall over the –"

Laundry. Yes. I pick myself out of the sheets.

"Put them on the chair. We can't have any more accidents."

"Mum, what's the matter?"

"Now listen, Katie, you're not to worry, but Zillah isn't well."

"Has she had another nosebleed?" But even as I ask I know it must be more serious than that.

"Yes. No. Well, she has, but it's not that exactly."

"Mum, what happened?"

"Doctor Stevens took blood tests a while ago because of all those nosebleeds Zillah was having. He's got some results back and now Zillah needs more tests, and they have to be done in hospital.

As it happens they had a bed available when he rang the hospital so she's gone in straight away. Janice was ringing from the hospital."

"What – to hospital? You mean she's gone to Truro?"

"Yes, I think so." Mum rubs her forehead distractedly. "I think Janice said Truro. It must have been Truro. Or was it? Anyway I've got her mobile number. She was in such a state, Katie, that I don't think she knew where she was herself. You know what Janice is about Zillah."

"But it was only a nosebleed. People don't go into hospital because of a nosebleed."

"It was the blood test results, apparently. Dr Stevens didn't get them phoned through to him until four o'clock, and then he couldn't get through to Janice. No one was answering the phone, apparently."

It was when we were serving the teas. The phone rang and rang but Janice wiped her floury hand across her face and said, "Let it ring for once, it won't be anything important, just some feed supplier for Geoff."

"So they didn't hear the results until they called him later because Zillah fainted."

"Zillah fainted? When?"

"Janice thought it was the heat. Dr Stevens was very good, he came up straight away."

Fear swirls inside me. It rises in my throat and makes a bitter taste in my mouth.

"Mum. What's wrong with Zillah?"

Mum rubs her forehead harder.

"We don't really know. Dr Stevens told Janice there were abnormalities in her blood count."

It sounds horrible, but I still don't understand what it means.

"Nor do I," says Mum, but from the way she looks I can see that she understands more than I do. But I don't want to ask her any more, because I don't want her to tell me. As long as I don't know, this can't really be happening.

CHAPTER ELEVEN

Mum lets me stay up. We sit in the garden until it's completely dark, and then Mum lights our little candle lantern. Mum gets out her old diaries and lets me read the one from the year she was eleven. I love reading Mum's old diaries because most of the time the person who wrote them seems completely different from Mum, and then there's a flash where she's just like Mum, only she's still a child.

June 5th 1978

Have decided to change my name. I don't know WHY my parents called me Maggie. Leonard Winterbottom calls me Magpie and I hate it! I much prefer the name Suzi and so do all my friends.

"Mum, was he really called Leonard Winterbottom?"

Imagine being called Leonard Winterbottom and daring to laugh at someone who was only called Maggie.

"What? Which bit are you reading? Oh, Leonard Winterbottom! Do you know, Katie, I met him again, about five years ago. He was working in a travel agency that specialized in winter sports," says Mum.

"Do you think he chose that job because of his name?"

We both laugh hysterically.

"Did he still try and call you Magpie?"

"He most certainly didn't. He wrote down his address, and he'd changed the spelling of his name."

"What to?"

"Winterbotham."

"I bet when he goes skiing he falls down on his winterbotham."

June 28th 1976

Thirty-eight days until my birthday, not counting today. 119 days til Christmas. Had sausages for tea!

"Mum, didn't anything ever happen to you when you were my age?"

"Of course it did," says Mum crossly. "Anyway, sausages were worth writing about, compared to most of the meals we had."

"What kind of food did your mother used to cook?"

I love hearing about this. My grandma worked in a pottery, making designs for plates and jugs. She certainly wasn't too interested in cooking, any more than Mum is.

"She cooked an ox tongue once," says Mum. "It was a huge blue thing with roots on it, and she had to simmer it in a preserving pan for hours. When it was cold she put a plate on top of it with an iron weight to press it down. And then the skin come off like a glove, with all the tongue bubbles on it—"

"Yuck, Mum, don't tell me any more—"

"And then she sliced it up and put it on plates with a tomato each. No one could eat it. After that she bought tins of Spam."

"What's Spam?"

"You don't want to know, Katie. Another thing my mother used to do was, when the bread was stale, she'd put the loaf under the cold tap and then bake it in the oven again. She said it tasted just the same as fresh bread."

"I'm so glad you don't do any cooking," I say. Mum looks hurt. "I mean, much cooking," I add hastily. "I love the – the Christmas pudding you cook."

That is safe, as Christmas only comes once a year and Mum buys our pudding from a health-food shop. Once I pretended to Mum that I liked the very lumpy porridge with golden syrup she made when I'd had flu, and she was so pleased I'd enjoyed it that she tried to make it every single morning. I had to bury the packet of porridge oats in the bottom of the dustbin, and make a slug trap out of the golden syrup.

• • •

Suddenly the flame in our candle lantern shrinks down. There is almost no candle left, only wax. The dark comes crowding in around us. I feel cold, although it isn't cold, and I shiver.

"Look up at those stars," says Mum.

The sky is thick with stars. The more I look the more I see, some of them clustering into constellations, others standing alone, sending out light to us that started out millions of years ago.

"I still can't get used to how bright they are," says Mum. "After all those years in London I'd almost forgotten about the stars."

Zillah's got a book about the stars. She knows lots of the constellations. One day she's going to get a proper telescope, the kind astronomers have.

"Do you think Zillah's asleep, Mum?"

"I expect so," says Mum. "Hospitals keep early hours. Everyone gets up early and goes to bed early. It's to do with the nurses' shifts."

"Zillah will hate that."

Zillah likes to read in bed. She sits up for hours sometimes, reading and reading. I should think she's read every single book in our school library. Our old school library. She'll be getting started on the secondary school library soon.

"Zillah's having more tests tomorrow, Katie. If the tests are all right, she might be home soon."

"She'll hate being in a ward with other people."

"It's probably a special children's ward."

"That's even worse." I can't imagine Zillah sleeping in a ward full of cots and pictures of bunny rabbits and cartoon princesses. I imagine her lying awake, pale and furious.

"Janice is with her. Geoff's got to get home for the milking, but Janice is staying overnight."

I can't say, "That's even worse," again. Janice is Mum's friend. But at home Zillah's got her bedroom to go to when she wants to get away from her mum. There won't be anywhere to escape from Janice in a hospital children's ward.

"I wish I could go and see her. Do you think I could phone her on Janice's mobile?"

"It's very late. She's probably asleep, and we don't want to disturb the other patients in the ward. Besides I don't think Janice would be using her mobile in the hospital. Mobiles interfere with some of the equipment."

This morning Zillah was walking up to Granny Carne's with me, free, just like we always were. Tonight she's a hospital patient. How can things change so quickly? If Zillah was well enough to climb to Granny Carne's, and be a waitress later on, and do everything she normally does, then why is she suddenly trapped in a hospital bed?

"Come on, Katie. It's past eleven."

When I am ready for bed I turn off my light and pull back my curtain and kneel on my bed so I can see the stars. Probably Zillah won't be asleep, and I wonder if she knows that I'm thinking of her.

Just before I fall asleep, in that time when the dreams you had the night before come crowding back, I tell myself, *Tomorrow things will be back to the way they were.* I hold on to the thought as sleep washes over me.

CHAPTER TWELVE

Acute lymphoblastic leukaemia (ALL) is a form of cancer that affects the lymphocyte-producing cells in the bone marrow. Lymphocytes are white blood cells that produce antibodies and are vital parts of the body's immune system.

I didn't understand what it meant either, the first time I read it. Mr T downloaded it all from the Internet for me. (He and Mrs T and the little Ts are back from holiday now.) Mr T also gave me some leaflets which are produced for families and friends of children who have acute lymphoblastic leukaemia.

Things have not gone back to the way they were. Zillah has acute lymphoblastic leukaemia. She hasn't got enough normal cells in her blood and that's why she was tired and breathless and had nosebleeds and fevers. You have to have enough healthy red blood cells and healthy white blood cells, but the cancer in Zillah's bone marrow is stopping her from producing them. Now she's got to take loads of drugs called chemotherapy and they will get rid of the cancerous cells, so that the normal ones can grow again. This is what it says in the leaflets, and Mum says it's true.

Zillah has had loads of tests. I'm not allowed to visit her yet because she might get an infection and it would be dangerous for her. Mr T has lent Zillah his laptop and he's let me borrow one of the school computers so that we can email. And there's a phone they wheel round the hospital wards.

When Janice first told Mum the results of Zillah's bone-marrow test (lots of bad cells and not enough good ones), I thought of two things:

1) Zillah will die

2) All Zillah's hair will fall out because of chemotherapy. That happened to a boy in my old class in London.

But Mum has explained to me that 1) isn't true. Nowadays about eighty per cent of children who get ALL recover. Every year more children recover because the treatment gets better.

Eighty per cent is four out of five.

Soon, Mum says, the treatment for ALL will be so good that everyone will survive. She shows me a graph with the survival statistics improving year by year.

But Zillah is not a statistic. Zillah is Zillah, the only one of her.

• • •

Zillah emailed me this morning about 2)

Mum brought me in a WIG CATALOGUE today! But I told her that even if ALL my hair falls out from the chemo I am most definitely not wearing a wig. I might wear a bandanna. Or my friends will just have to look at my bald head.

• • •

It's quite hard to imagine Zillah without her hair. Her hair is thick and wild and dark and it's like part of her character. But I could easily imagine the dialogue between Zillah and Janice.

JANICE: (pointing to picture in wig catalogue) This one's nice Zillah – quite realistic!

ZILLAH: I'm going to be bald, Mum. I'm not covering it up to make other people feel better. Get used to it!

• • •

This morning I was in the post office.

"How's Zillah?" asked Mrs Pascoe. "Is there any more news?"

"She's started chemo," I said.

"I heard she's up in Bristol."

"It's the specialist unit," I said. "It's the best place."

There was a rustling noise behind me and Mrs Delabole came out from behind the boiled sweets.

"Leukaemia, she's got, isn't it," she said gloomily. "Cancer of the blood. Well, they've got to do what they can. Got to keep hope alive," and she lumbered up to the counter with her Everton Mints and Winter Candy. She held out a five-pound note, but to my surprise Mrs Pascoe didn't take it. Instead, she folded her arms and glared at Mrs Delabole.

"That's pure ignorance, that is," she said. "With modern medicine Zillah'll be back out in that boat of hers again by the end of the summer, and don't you come in my shop saying otherwise, Charity Delabole."

Mrs Delabole huffed and snorted. I thought she was going to argue, but probably she remembered that nowhere else in the village sells Everton mints. She took her change, snapped it into her purse, and went out without saying goodbye.

"People get frightened of the word cancer," said Mrs Pascoe. "They don't know what to say. But if they've nothing better to say than that, they should keep their mouths shut. Help yourself to a Crunchie, Katie. They're your favourite, aren't they?"

"Thanks," I said.

"I've had it, you know," said Mrs Pascoe. "Chemo. Cancer. And here I am. You tell Zillah to keep fighting."

Everyone wants Zillah to fight, which is quite funny really when you think how much trouble Zillah usually gets into for being fierce and Zillah-ish.

Imagine grumpy, lumpy old Mrs Delabole being called Charity. I must tell Zillah.

• • •

email from Katie to Zillah

I am still sitting over the blank screen when Mum comes out of her studio.

"What're you doing, Katie?"

"Sending an email to Zillah."

"Give her my love."

Mum steps lightly around the kitchen, filling the kettle, putting it on the stove.

"She'll be glad to hear from you. It must be very boring for her in there."

"Mum."

"What?"

"Nothing."

Mum stops and looks over my shoulder at the screen.

"But you haven't written anything, Katie."

"I know. I can't think what to say. Everything I start to write seems stupid, when she's –"

"When she's what?"

"When she's in hospital and she might die."

There's a long silence. At last Mum says, "Did you understand what I told you about recovery rates?"

"Yes. But that still leaves twenty per cent. What if Zillah's in the twenty per cent?"

"We have to believe that she won't be," says Mum.

"I do most of the time, but sometimes I can't."

"I know. But we have to. Zillah has got to feel that you believe it."

On the screen the cursor winks softly.

"Do you think it would be OK if I wrote about *Wayfarer*? Or would it make her feel sad?"

"I think she'd like it. You went down to check

Wayfarer last night, didn't you?"

"Yes. Zillah asked me to bring her right up on the shingle."

"Tell her you've done it."

Dear Zillah

I've brought Wayfarer right up to the top of the beach, like you said, and she's under the tarpaulin. I could put her in the boathouse if you want. Mark and Bry said they'd come over and help.

I think having a wig would be stupid, because you aren't going to be bald for long enough.

Loads of people send their love. I gave Mark your email address and Susie Buryan asked for it too so I'm afraid you might get a long and boring email from her about the Guide camp she went to last week. Mrs Pascoe said to tell you she sends her very best and she is getting in some of those toffees you like and will send them with your mum at the first opportunity. The little Ts have done you a painting of a fox eating their chickens (yes, it's happened again). Mr T is going to scan it into his computer and email it to you. It's pretty scary.

I can't wait until they let me see you. I haven't got a cough or a cold or anything. Mum says she'll drive me up in the van when I'm allowed to visit. She's got two new front tyres so we're all ready to go.

Rose|

The cursor winks again. Zillah doesn't want to know about Rose. I press delete, and Rose's name is wiped away.

CHAPTER THIRTEEN

The phone rings, and it's Zillah.

"Katie?"

"Zillah! Are you OK?"

"Yeah, I'm fine."

She's in hospital, she can't see visitors apart from Janice and Geoff and she's having chemotherapy. Even reading the names of the chemotherapy drugs on the Internet makes me feel scared. I feel as if Zillah has disappeared into another world, and there's no door I can go through to find her. But this is not what Zillah and I talk about.

Tonight she wants to tell me about how she's won the latest battle in the war of Whose Body Is It Anyway.

The war of Whose Body Is It Anyway began the moment Zillah went into hospital. Zillah hates being told what to do.

Now, we'll just pop this wrist-band on you ... another blood test, just a little prick ... we need you to wee into this container...

Hospitals are about telling people to do things. Zillah had to have all kinds of tests straight away. In one of them the doctors had to take a sample of her bone marrow to check for cancerous cells. Zillah and I agreed that this sounded gross, but in fact it wasn't too bad because Zillah had an anaesthetic so she didn't feel anything.

"The doctor came to talk about my chemo today," says Zillah now. "All in words of one syll-ab-le. And she kept on smiling. And then I realized that she'd already talked to Mum and Dad before she talked to me, because of the way Mum was watching me instead of listening. It was so annoying. I'm the one that's got cancer, not them."

"I hate it when people do that," I agree. My voice comes out small and tight and I wish I could make it normal.

"So I asked the doctor to explain it properly," Zillah goes on. Her voice sounds bright and fierce and very Zillah-ish. "We've been doing science in school since we were four years old, so I should be able to understand some of it. And I've been looking on leukaemia websites, so I know some of the words. Just because I'm young, it doesn't mean I'm stupid. Plenty of adults are stupider than me."

This is certainly true. Zillah isn't that great at school work, because she doesn't bother, but she has read thousands of books and is the only one in our class who can understand Mr T when he goes off into a rap about economic conditions in Yakutsk.

"Did you tell her that? About some adults being stupider than you?"

"Yes."

"What did she say?"

"She didn't have time to say anything, because Mum started. *The doctor's busy, Zillah, she hasn't got time to answer all your questions.* Mum thinks all doctors are like God, only better, and she doesn't want me to know anything. She thinks I'll get scared. *Just lie there like a good girl, Zill, and the doctors'll make you better*, that's Mum's attitude. She even says the word *doctor* as if it's holy. But it's me that's ill, not Mum, and it's Mum who's got the attitude problem, not me. I told Mum that I wasn't having any more treatment unless I understood it. I'm not a laboratory animal."

Wow. Imagine daring to say that in front of a doctor. I wouldn't be able to, no matter how much I wanted to. I'd be too embarrassed. And then, after the doctor had gone, I'd lie there feeling angry with myself for being so pathetic. Zillah's way was better, but maybe you had to be Zillah to do it –

"Did the doctor explain the treatment?"

"Yeah, she did. She was good. She said to Mum, maybe she'd like to get a coffee in the dayroom, and so Mum went off, even though I could see she didn't want to. Then the doctor sat on the bed and told me properly about how the drugs work. I didn't understand before. Some of them destroy the cancerous cells and some of them stop my kidneys being affected by the other drugs. If they work I'll go into remission. I'm in the remission induction stage now."

It's so strange to hear Zillah talking about it in that way, so grown-up and detached, as if she and the doctor are partners.

"Chemo works in over eighty per cent of cases," she says.

"I know," I say, clutching the phone with hands that were suddenly sticky with fear. A hundred take away eighty still leaves twenty.

"Don't be scared, Katie," says Zillah. "I hate it when people get scared."

"I'm not. I know you're going to be OK," I say quickly.

"It's hard with Mum," says Zillah. "She's scared all the time. She thinks I can't tell. And she's here all the time, too. The other parents go off into town sometimes, but Mum won't." Zillah sighs. "You know Mum."

I can hear Janice as clearly as if Zillah were playing a tape of her. *You haven't eaten your yoghurt, Zill. You've got to eat, or you won't keep your strength up. I could make you a milky drink instead if you like. What about doing a puzzle to take your mind off things? You used to like doing puzzles. You can't read in this light, Zill, you'll damage your eyes.*

"Mum keeps saying how wonderful the hospital is because they let parents stay with their children twenty-four hours a day, and they've even got little bedrooms for them." Zillah sighs again. "The nurses keep saying to Mum, *Why don't you go out for a couple of hours, do some shopping or go to a café?* But Mum won't. She thinks I'll die if she goes out of the room."

The word "die" slips into our conversation as if it belongs there, although we've never said it before. Everyone talks about remission and survival. No one talks about dying.

• • •

So I ask Zillah what else has been happening today.

"I saw the teacher from the hospital school. She thinks I could combine maths and computing and do some spreadsheets. I told her about us doing the accounts for Mum's cream tea business. She reckoned it would be much more efficient to do it on the computer."

"But Zillah, it's the school holidays!"

"I know. But guess what? Parents don't stay while the teacher's with you."

"Excellent," I say, and this time my voice comes out right.

• • •

"Poor Janice," says Mum thoughtfully, when I tell her about the milky drinks, jigsaw puzzles and Janice not leaving Zillah for a minute.

"Poor Zillah, you mean."

"No, Katie, at the moment it's Janice I feel most sorry for."

"But it's Zillah who's ill."

"Yes, I know."

Mum doesn't say any more. She has made some chicken soup by boiling the bones of an old chicken all day and throwing in some chunks of potato and carrot. When she tasted it she thought it needed some extra flavour so she sprinkled curry powder on top.

"I was going to make lasagne, Mum."

"Oh dear, don't you like the soup, Katie?"

"Um, it's very nice, Mum –"

"I've decided I'm going to do more cooking. It's not fair to leave it all to you."

"But I like cooking, Mum!"

"Yes, I know you do, but . . . well, I just don't want to take you for granted, that's all."

And to my amazement, Mum puts down her soup spoon and her eyes are full of tears.

"Mum! What is it, Mum? What's the matter?" Mum reaches over and takes my hand.

"Don't cry, Mum."

"I'm not crying, Katie. I'm just so glad –" she swallows – "that you're all right. And then I feel terrible. Poor Janice..."

"I know."

And suddenly, just for a second, I see Janice as if she's just a person, not a parent who does all the irritating parent things she can possibly do. And I can believe that she and Mum were once girls the same age as Zillah and me, and that they were best friends.

"Mum, will you promise me something?"

"What is it?"

"You won't ever make that chicken soup again?"

• • •

There isn't time to do lasagne, so I make us pasta with tomato sauce while Mum finishes the drawing of *Wayfarer* she's doing for Zillah to stick on her hospital locker. While we eat, I tell Mum about the email Zillah had from Susie Buryan yesterday.

"She told Zillah not to worry about going bald, because it's the inside of a person that counts, not the outside. That's what God sees."

"Oh dear."

"Zill is going to tell Susie I'm shaving my hair off in sympathy, and is Susie going to do the same."

"Katie! You are not going to shave your hair off—"

"Mum. Please. It was a joke."

Mum runs her finger through her hair distractedly, then she pushes the drawing of *Wayfarer* across to me.

"Do you think Zillah will like it?"

Mum has drawn *Wayfarer* slipping through the entrance of the cove where Zillah keeps the boat. The water is deep and black and the rocks are high on either side. Zillah is carefully manoeuvring *Wayfarer* into open water. Her expression is concentrated as she glances side-ways to judge the distance between her oar and the rock.

"It's exactly how Zillah looks when she's taking *Wayfarer* out," I say.

"I went down to the boat-cove to do some sketches, at low tide," Mum says. "First of all I took the tarpaulin off *Wayfarer* and made a sketch, but when it was finished I didn't think Zillah would like it. *Wayfarer* looked abandoned, somehow, up on the shingle. You know how sad boats can look when they're out of the water. Then I remembered that we'd got those photos you took of Zillah rowing. So I climbed round on the rocks to make some sketches of the entrance of the cove, and then I brought them back and worked from the sketches and the photos."

"It's exactly how Zillah looks when she's rowing," I say. I can just imagine Mum scrambling over rocks and limpets and sharp mussel shells at low tide, with her sketchbook and charcoal pencils. And then perching on a wet, seaweedy rock to make her sketches. Nothing is too much trouble for Mum when she's doing a drawing. Lucky she didn't get so absorbed in drawing that she forgot the time and got cut off by the incoming tide. Lucky she didn't fall. . .

"You won't go out on those rocks again, will you, Mum? They're so slippery, and if you fell no one would be there to help you. You're always telling me and Zill to stick together down there."

"I was extremely careful, Katie," says Mum indignantly. "You seem to forget that I spent every summer holiday down here when I was a child."

"What about those scars on your legs then? The ones you got when you fell off that rock when you were eleven?"

"Yes, well, a few scars are worth it, for all the good times we had. We used to be out from after breakfast until teatime, me and Janice, climbing and swimming and surfing down at St Ives—"

"Did you surf, Mum? I didn't know that."

"Oh yes, Janice and I had our own surfboards. Not like the ones they have these days, though. Ours were made of plywood."

"Plywood! I bet they were rubbish."

"They were not rubbish, Katie. They used to hire out wooden boards on Porthmeor, painted bright blue so you couldn't walk off with them. Oh, we had a wonderful time."

"Like me and Zillah," I say thoughtfully. And suddenly I miss Zillah so much. It's only half-past seven and it's still light and warm. If Zillah was at home, instead of in hospital, I'd probably phone her. We'd go out – maybe up to the village, maybe down to the cove, maybe along the cliffs to watch the seals. Or we might just stay in my bedroom or Zillah's bedroom, talking and listening to music and eating leftover cake from Janice's teas.

It's a perfect evening but it hangs in front of me, empty. As if she has heard my thoughts, Mum says, "It's still early. Shall we go up to the pub and have a Coke?"

"Mm, yes, that'd be nice," I say, trying to sound enthusiastic in order not to hurt Mum's feelings. Usually it's a treat to go and sit in the pub garden and have coke and crisps. But, apart from the tourists, everyone who comes in the pub knows Zillah and her family. They will all ask how Zillah is, and tonight I don't want to talk about it.

"Or why don't you go up to the caravan park and see Rose?" suggests Mum.

CHAPTER FOURTEEN

But there's something I've got to do first. I go up to my bedroom and look at my hair-wrap in the mirror. It looks just as good as it did when Rose first wrapped it. I am sure that I can take off the silver bread without unravelling the rest of the wrap. The lucky bead. But it's not as easy as it looks. Rose has fixed the bead in so tight that I can't undo it without –

"Mum! Can I borrow your scissors?"

Scissors in hand, I try again. If I just snip this little bit of thread here, I'm sure the silver bead will slip out –

But again it doesn't. It's as if Rose has fixed it with superglue. The long silver bead with its mysterious pattern of unreadable writing doesn't want to separate itself from my hair. I snip again, and the scissors click on air.

It's because I'm trying to cut out the bead while I'm looking in the mirror. The mirror reflects everything backwards, so the scissors are in the wrong place when I snip.

I stare in the mirror at the strand of hair Rose has wrapped. Honey and buttercup and pale, sunshiny yellow, with the silver bead shining. Suddenly I don't want to spoil it. It looks so good and I'll never be able to wrap it again like that. Of course it isn't really a lucky bead. Rose was just saying that. It won't make any difference to Zillah if she has my lucky bead or not. It's the chemo that's going to make her better, not magic. And Zillah doesn't even know that I was thinking of giving her the bead, so she won't be hurt if I don't. She liked my hair-wrap, she wouldn't want me to spoil it.

But in the mirror my face is going red, and I can't meet my own eyes.

I close my eyes. I lift Mum's sharp, bright scissors. I feel for the hair-wrap and lift it away from the rest of my hair. I take a deep breath and now my eyes are squeezed so tight shut they hurt. I open the scissors wide and cut.

There's a click on the floor as the bead falls. And not just the bead. My beautiful hair-wrap has gone. I've cut it halfway up by mistake, slicing off the bead and the best part of Rose's intricate pattern of honey and sunshine and gold.

A strand of hair sticks out of my head, with threads unravelling from it. On the floor there is the rest of my wrapped hair, with the silver bead.

Mum will go crazy, especially after what I said earlier about cutting off my hair. Quickly, I pick up the fallen strand of hair and cut off the bead, which comes away easily now. I throw the hair and wrapping into my bin, and then I start pulling off the part of the wrap which is still attached to my head. Rose has wrapped my hair so tightly that I have to tug much harder than I want to, and the threads come off with my hairs caught in them. It really hurts.

When all the wrapping is off I get my hairbrush and brush my hair down so that the cut-off part won't show any more. But it doesn't work. I wish I had wild, bushy hair like Zillah's, where a cut-off strand wouldn't show, but mine is smooth and dark and shiny and the shorter bit of hair sticks out jaggedly. Maybe if I trim it, it will look better. I pick up Mum's scissors again and try to smooth off the ends, but accidentally another long strand gets caught in the scissors and that comes off too. It looks worse than ever and now I'm starting to panic. Mum is bound to notice. And everyone else will notice as well. Maybe I should cut all my hair level with the short bit. But I can't do that, because I can't reach round the back of myself, and I have never seen a hairstyle with short hair at the front and long hair at the back.

I turn away from the mirror in despair. But there's the silver bead, glowing on the shelf under the mirror. It looks brighter than ever in the evening light, and the writing on it looks clearer. I pick it up and take it to the window and it flashes in the evening sunlight. The marks of writing on the bead are so clear, much sharper and brighter than they were when Rose first put it into my hair. I still can't read the message, but I am sure that the writing wants to be read.

Suddenly a solution to the hair problem occurs to me. If I wet my hair a bit it will all flatten down and Mum won't notice the cut-off bit.

Put water on my hair, comb it through, get some

bubble wrap and an envelope and stamp from Mum, carefully pack up the bead and write a note to Zillah, then seal the envelope and write her names and the hospital address. I can post it tomorrow.

"You're not going out with that wet hair, are you, Katie?"

"Oh – um, no, it's not really wet, it just got a bit damp when I washed my face."

Mum looks at me oddly. "Why didn't you use the hair-dryer?"

"Got to hurry Mum – got to get to Rose's before she goes to bed –"

"I doubt that Rose goes to bed at ten-past eight," Mum points out. "Don't be more than an hour, Katie."

"When I've got my mobile, you'll never have to worry about me!"

But I'm forgetting the new notice hanging at the top of the farm lane on the main road: CREAM TEAS CLOSED UNTIL FURTHER NOTICE DUE TO ILLNESS. Zillah and I are not earning any money now. Trainers and mobile will have to wait.

CHAPTER FIFTEEN

Just got back, so late that Mum started shouting about how it was nearly dark and she'd said only one hour, and she'd thought she could trust me.

Mum never shouts at me.

"It's *quarter to ten*, Katie. I don't want you roaming round the lanes on your own at this time of night, when it's getting dark!"

On my own. Of course, that's why Mum's scared. Usually I'm with Zillah.

I have had to promise that I'll wear my watch every time I go out, and I'll be back on time.

And now I'm waiting. Mum will go to bed soon, and I'll get into bed and turn out my light and then I'll listen until I hear the gravel patter against my window.

• • •

When I got to the caravan park I couldn't see Rose at first. Leah and Jesse were sitting drinking beers by the van. And wasn't that Jesse's brother Nathaniel with them? But surely he wouldn't come back here, not when Geoff had chased him off with a shotgun last time.

It was Nathaniel, and he saw me looking. He waved

his beer bottle and shouted, "Hey, you're Rose's friend, right?"

I thought he was going to tell me where Rose was, but he didn't, and I didn't want to ask. I don't like talking to Jesse, or his brother. I can see why Rose doesn't like Jesse. He looks at you in a mocking way, as if he knows something you don't.

There was Great-Gran's sofa by the stream as always. The back of the sofa was towards me, but I could see Great-Gran's head, and beside her, another head. Rose.

They were sitting together, wrapped in one of Great-Gran's crocheted shawls. Rose sat very close to her great-gran. It looked almost as if they were huddling together out of danger, on the little island of the blue velvet sofa.

"Hi, Rose."

"Hi, Katie."

The shawl was tucked right up to Rose's chin, although it was a warm night. I wondered if they were going to sleep out there.

"Come and sit down," Rose said. She and Great-Gran moved up and made space for me, and unfolded some of the shawl for me. The colours were beautiful. Lilac and mauve and hyacinth and violet, softly shading into one another like the sky after sunset.

"My great-gran made it," said Rose proudly. "She used to make shawls and sell them."

Great-Gran smiled and her gums showed. She wasn't wearing her teeth, and her voice was mumbly as she said, "You can't get colours like these in the shops."

"Katie, did you see my mum and Jesse?" said Rose in a low voice.

"Yes, they're over by the van. And—"

"I know. He's back. He came this afternoon."

"Trouble," said Great-Gran, and sucked her gums sharply. Then she reached down to her table, fumbled for her teeth, and slipped them in.

"Why has he come back?" I asked. "There'll be trouble if Geoff – if Mr Treliske sees Jesse's brother back on his land."

"My mum doesn't want him here," said Rose. "He came without asking. Jesse's different, when Nathaniel's here. I don't like it."

I looked over at the group by the van. Jesse's head was thrown back and he was laughing loudly. Other campers were noticing him and Nathaniel. I thought of what Great-Gran had said: *trouble*.

"Jesse's no good," said Great-Gran. "Why our Leah took up with him, I'll never know. All he's given her is babies."

"I don't like them," Rose said. "I don't want to stay here with them."

And to my amazement Great-Gran turned to Rose and said, "You've got money, girl. You don't have to stay. You can go where you choose."

But Rose is only twelve years old, I wanted to say. How can she go where she chooses? Of course she's got to stay with her mum … hasn't she?

"It's not a fit home for you, girl, not with those two young pikers about," went on Great-Gran. I didn't know what a piker was, but I guessed she meant Jesse and Nathaniel. Slowly and thoughtfully, Rose nodded.

"You got your money safe, Rose?" asked Great-Gran.

"I got it safe," said Rose.

"Then you add this to it, girl," said Great-Gran, and she leaned forward and opened her secret box. I didn't see inside it, but I saw the flash of banknotes as she passed folded money to Rose.

"I'll pay it back to you, Great-Gran," said Rose.

"No need," said Great-Gran. "No need. And Katie'll make my tea, won't you? Now that she's learned the art of it."

It was getting dusk as I made the tea. We'd been talking longer than I'd realized, and I knew Mum would be getting worried.

"I'll come down to yours, Katie," said Rose, when I'd carried the steaming tea carefully to Great-Gran. "Not now, later on. I'll come when everyone's gone to sleep, and I'll throw up gravel on your window so you know it's me. My mum and Jesse and Nathaniel are leaving at first light, and they won't stop to look for me."

"But then where will you go?"

"Over to Newlyn. My friend's there, the one I told you about. Marijke. I sent her a message with one of the girls who does henna tattoos down at the harbour, and Marijke sent me a message back. She wants me to come. I told you, she's my friend. I can stay with her for the rest of the summer. I'll get a bus over in the morning."

"But Rose, what about your mum?"

Rose shrugged. "You've seen my mum. She'll be all

right. I'll find her again at the end of the summer. She'll be needing some of what I've made to help her get through the winter."

"You mean you'll give her your money?"

"Long as I've got enough to get by, I will," said Rose. "She's got Titus and the babies to look after."

"But won't she be scared something's happened to you?"

"She'll hear where I am fast enough. She won't come running after me. She knows I'm all right with Marijke."

Great-Gran patted Rose's hand. "You've got a smart head on you, Rose," she said. "You've got it all worked out."

"You'll be all right, won't you, Gran?" asked Rose.

"That Nathaniel and your mum's Jesse, they lifted my sofa between them meek as lambs when I wanted it turned," said Great-Gran with satisfaction. "And I have it in my mind that Nathaniel may be a hand with the tea-making."

Everything is backwards in Rose's family, like trying to cut your hair while you're looking in the mirror. Rose is only my age – well, a few months older – and she can go where she wants and pay for her own life and decide who she lives with. Jesse and Nathaniel are hard enough to frighten Rose, but soft enough to be bossed around by Great-Gran. Leah is Rose's mum, but she doesn't look after her, and Rose doesn't seem to expect her to.

"You lost my lucky bead," said Rose suddenly, as she walked with me towards the gate. "You took your hair-wrap out."

"I didn't lose it exactly –"

"What did you do with it then?"

"I posted it to Zillah in hospital."

"The luck was for you, not for her," said Rose.

"Well, Zillah's got it now," I lied, knowing that the envelope was lying in the red postbox at the top of the farm lane. But I wouldn't put it past Rose to get it out somehow, if I told her.

"Zillah's your real friend, isn't she?" asked Rose, and now she didn't sound sure of herself at all. Or maybe it was just that people's voices sound lonely when it's growing dark.

"She's my best friend," I said, "but you're my friend as well."

"She's lucky," said Rose.

"She's in hospital with cancer," I pointed out.

"Her mum or her dad is there with her all the time, you said so. You'd be there all the time if they let you. Every time I go into the village I hear them talking about her. Zillah, Zillah, Zillah. Mum says they were even talking about Zillah in the pub last night. They're going to have a Quiz Night to raise money for the Treliskes to have a holiday, once she's out of hospital."

"Well ... Zillah belongs here. Her family have always lived here."

"I know," said Rose. "And now she's got my lucky bead too."

"Rose ... you know the writing on it? Does it sometimes come clearer, so you can read it?"

Rose glanced at me quickly and I could tell she knew

what I meant, but she said nothing. I thought of what Zillah had said. Beads from Abyssinia . . . beads from Babylon.

"Rose, where does the lucky bead come from? Where did you find it?"

But Rose shook her head. "It wouldn't be lucky any more, Katie, if I told you."

• • •

There's a little sound in the dark. A footstep. It goes through me with a fizz like electricity, and I sit bolt upright in bed. There's a little patter on the window, like rain. Gravel on the glass. It's Rose. Noiselessly I slide up the window.

"Rose, wait by the door. I'm coming down. Don't make a sound, Mum's sleeping."

CHAPTER SIXTEEN

Rose has brought her glittery box of threads and beads, a backpack the same size as the one I take to school, and a rolled-up sleeping-bag.

"Is that all the stuff you're taking?"

"All I need," says Rose, and grins. "They think I'm asleep. Gran told them I'd been sick and I'd gone to bed in the back of the van with the little ones. Nathaniel's off down the pub with Jesse, and Mum's sleeping in the tent. They'll pack up and go at first light."

"But then they'll see you're not there."

"Mum'll find my note," says Rose. "I told you, Katie, she'll know I'm OK. And Jesse and Nathaniel won't care if I'm there or not, except for the money. Jesse can't make money like I do."

It sounds terrible. Is Rose telling the truth? Doesn't Jesse care about her at all, not even enough to worry if something bad might have happened to her? I know he's not her dad, but he is her stepdad. In a way. He must care about her a bit.

"No," says Rose. "He cares about my mum, and a bit about the babies and Titus, as long as they don't stop him doing what he wants to do."

"But he's your – your stepfather. He should look after you."

Rose doesn't just smile when I say this. She laughs. "He should do a lot of things," she says. I don't really understand what she means but I don't like to say so. Sometimes Rose makes me feel that I don't understand anything about life.

"Your dad really loved you, didn't he," says Rose.

"Yes."

"And he's dead. So that means you'll never have to ask yourself if he's stopped loving you. He'll always love you."

She says it in the strangest way, as if she's not sorry for me because Dad died. As if she's envious. As if it's a good thing to die, because then nothing can change.

But it's not. I know that.

"I'll lay my sleeping-bag out on the floor," says Rose.

"No, I'll sleep on the floor. You're the guest."

"Don't be stupid. I can sleep anywhere," says Rose proudly, and she lays out her sleeping-bag on the floor and clambers into it. She zips it tight up to her neck and stares up at the ceiling and sighs.

"It's nice here," she says. "Really nice. Peaceful. You sure your mum won't wake up, Katie?"

"Even if she does, she won't come in my room."

"Night then."

"Night, Rose."

We fall asleep straight away, at least I do. But I wake suddenly in the middle of the night, from a bad dream. The dream is something about Zillah and I don't want to think about it or remember it. I feel hot and sweaty and I'm breathing fast, as if I've been running. The room isn't completely dark, but when I pull back my curtain it is moonlight, not morning. The moon is full. Everything is bright but strange, and it makes me shiver. Suddenly I remember about Rose. I turn to look at where she's sleeping, but she's not asleep at all. She is sitting up in her sleeping-bag, her hands clasped around her knees.

"Rose?"

"Yeah."

"Are you all right?"

"Just waiting for the morning," says Rose.

"Can't you sleep?"

"No. I can't sleep in houses. I feel like the walls are coming in on me. You had a bad dream, didn't you?"

"How do you know?"

"I heard you. You were saying, *No, no*. What were you dreaming about?"

In the dead of night it's easy to talk.

"About Zillah," I said. "But I can't remember it properly."

"I wonder if she's awake now," says Rose. "Maybe that's why you were dreaming about her. She was in your dream because she was thinking about you."

I try to imagine what the hospital is like, but I keep seeing long rows of white beds and I know it's not really like that at all. I've never been in hospital.

"I wish I could go and see her," I say.

"Why can't you?"

"Because of infections. The chemo does something to

her immune system. If she catches a cold or chickenpox or something she'd be really ill."

"Sounds bad," says Rose, in a voice that says she doesn't want to think about it. Because she's thinking about the morning coming, and first light, and her mum and Jesse and Nathaniel and all of them going off in the van. Suddenly I wonder if Rose even knows where they are going. And Rose will be going over to Penzance on the bus, and then to Newlyn, on her own...

"Rose?"

"Yeah?"

"Has Marijke got a mobile?

"I don't know. Why?"

"I was going to say, you could ring her from our phone. just to check she's there."

"I know she's there," says Rose. "I told you, Marijke knows I'm coming."

Rose is tough. Much tougher than me. She doesn't go to school, she doesn't live in one place, she earns her own money, she's free –

But she's been lying awake. Sitting up awake, I mean. Even for Rose there must be something frightening about leaving your mum and your whole family, and going off on your own to stay with someone who isn't even related to you. Even if Marijke's as nice as Rose says she is.

• • •

Rose doesn't seem to want to talk any more. I pull the duvet up around my head and try to send myself back to sleep. But even my best way of going to sleep (imagining a desert island with blue water lapping and lapping endlessly on the sand) doesn't work. I count the waves until they get to a hundred and ninety-seven, and then I sit up, too. Inside me, something has been decided. I can't let Rose go off alone to catch the eight o'clock bus to Penzance.

"Rose?"

"What?"

"I'm coming with you."

"You're crazy. Marijke can't take two of us. Her tent isn't big enough."

I am amazed that Rose even thinks for a second that I might want to run away from Mum and live in a tent with her and Marijke.

"I don't mean to stay. I'll go over to Penzance with you on the bus, and it's only a mile or so down to Newlyn from there. We can walk."

"And then what'll you do?"

"Get the bus back."

"You really are crazy, Katie."

"No, I'm not. If you go on your own and you don't arrive, no one would ever know. Marijke would just think you'd changed your mind."

"Of course I'll arrive."

"I know. But … just in case, Rose. You shouldn't go on your own so early."

"You'll be on your own, coming back."

"It'll be all right then. There'll be loads of people around. And Mum would know if I didn't come back. I'll leave her a note to say I've gone to Penzance to get a present for Zillah."

Never in a zillion years will Mum believe that I would get up in time to catch the early bus to Penzance on a school-holiday morning, just because I wanted to buy a present. However, Rose doesn't know that, and I can think about what to say to Mum later. And Mum doesn't know anything yet, because she's fast asleep. A picture of Mum, fast asleep and peaceful, comes into my mind. I push it out. I've got to make sure Rose is all right, and I can feel guilty about Mum later.

"All right," says Rose, grudgingly, as if she's doing me a big favour.

And that's it. I've got to do it now. It was all my idea, and that gives me the strangest feeling, because usually the ideas are mine and Zillah's, shared. We're together, carrying them out. Don't think of that. Think of Rose safe in Marijke's tent, and me coming home on the bus, knowing that Rose is with someone who will look after her. Or look after her a bit, anyway.

I lie down again and this time I'm asleep before the first blue wave reaches my island.

CHAPTER SEVENTEEN

"Katie? Is that you?"

I freeze on the stairs. Above me, Rose melts back into my bedroom.

"What is it, Mum?"

"What time is it?"

Mum's voice is thick with sleep.

"Um – only half-past seven. Just going out to the toilet, Mum."

For the first time in my life, I am glad that we have got an outside toilet, which is the perfect excuse to be creaking down the stairs at any hour of the day or night. I wait, but Mum doesn't answer. Maybe she's already fallen asleep again. Soundlessly, Rose creeps out on to the narrow landing between my bedroom and Mum's. Like a cat, she tiptoes down our old, squeaky cottage stairs without making a single creak.

I leave the note I've written for Mum on the kitchen table, folding it carefully and trying not to think of Mum's worried face when she unfolds it.

Dear Mum

I have gone on the bus to Penzance, to buy a present for Zillah. I'm sorry I did not tell you but it's a secret. I will phone you from a call box when we get there.

Lots and lots of love from Katie XXXX

PS PLEASE PLEASE don't get worried.

And then I slide back the bolt on the kitchen door and Rose and I are out in the early blue morning.

On our way.

We hurry up the farm lane, past the farmhouse, keeping close to the hedge in case Zillah's dad is out doing his early jobs and he sees us. Past the entrance to the caravan park. . .

Rose is right. They've gone. There are patches of pale yellow grass where the van was, and the tent. It's too far away to see if there's another pale yellow patch by the stream, where Great-Gran's blue velvet sofa stood. I stare at the calm grey-green early-morning field, and it's hard to believe that the blue velvet sofa was ever there at all. If Rose wasn't with me, I could easily believe that Great-Gran and her sofa had been a dream.

"What are you staring at?" asks Rose. "I told you they'd be off. They'll have left at first light."

I think of how glad Geoff will be. His field is back the way he likes it, with a few holidaymakers in neat tents and cream caravans. He won't be able to believe his luck.

But Janice will worry about the babies. Janice didn't think Leah looked after the babies properly.

"Mind, I don't want to be hard on her, she has her hands full with twins."

I can just hear Janice's voice, but she's not here. She's in the hospital, probably already asking Zillah if she wants a nice game of Snap. Hospital days begin early, Mum says—

"Katie, we'll miss that bus!"

Rose sounds anxious now, for the first time since I've known her.

"I'm coming." It must be horrible for Rose to see those pale yellow patches of grass, like a sign that reads, *We went without you. We didn't wait for you.*

Why couldn't they wait? Why didn't they go looking for Rose? Mum would never, ever leave me, no matter how angry she was. I think of Leah in the driving seat, with her strong arms pulling the wheel, and Jesse and Nathaniel beside her. You can get three in a row in the front of their van. And where would they put Great-Gran? Maybe she would be in the back with the babies and Titus. Maybe she would still be perched on her sofa, on top of the van, drinking tea like the Queen.

But Rose says nothing. Her face is set. She won't cry and she won't smile. Rose is certainly tough.

• • •

Our bus rattles the twisty miles to Penzance. The bus driver didn't ask any awkward questions when we got on. He just grunted and said we were early birds. Rose said we were going shopping in Penzance, and that was that. I went red and said nothing.

I wonder if Mum's up yet. I wonder if she's taking her Chinese dressing gown off the back of the door, and going downstairs in bare feet, yawning the way she always does until she's had her first cup of coffee. And then she'll see my note, on the kitchen table.

It doesn't take long to get to Penzance. We bounce along the road, so high up we can see over all the hedges, and suddenly there's the town with its grey heap of slate roofs, and St Michael's Mount shining out in the bay. Rose gets up and walks to the front of the bus to talk to the driver, even though there's a notice that says you're not to distract him. But he doesn't seem to mind. He laughs, and Rose laughs, and then she comes back to her seat.

"We don't need to walk," she says, "There's another bus into Newlyn. It goes ten minutes after ours arrives."

And she's right. Our driver points out the Newlyn bus, which is waiting with its engine running. Rose jumps down with a neat, confident flick of her hand to say goodbye, and I hurry after her, trip on the step and nearly fall flat on the Tarmac.

In the second bus, Rose gets a scrap of paper out of her jeans pocket and peers at it.

"Four, Nankavees Cottages," she reads carefully. "Is that right, Katie?"

"Yes, that's right."

It is spelled wrong, but I don't say anything because I am sure it is Rose's spelling.

"That's good," says Rose, satisfied. "I wasn't sure I got it down right when Marijke told me."

"But I thought Marijke lived in a tent."

"She does. She's in a field outside town, but the cottage is where I'm meeting her. I'm going to ask the driver where the art place is. The cottage is near there."

We're in Newlyn. The bus is slowing, and the driver turns around and shouts, "Art gallery is down that street there if you two girls still want it."

We are out in the grey, quiet streets. Rose looks up and down them, frowning. I remember what she said about not wanting to sleep in houses because it felt as if the walls were coming in on her. Suddenly I see the cottages through Rose's eyes. Small windows, narrow doors. Like little prisons.

There is a sign on the wall that reads Nankervis Cottages.

"There you are, Rose. It's the right place."

Rose frowns more deeply, peering at the sign.

"You sure it's the right one, Katie?"

"Yes. We've only got to find number four now."

But this is not as easy as it sounds. The cottage numbers jump from one to three.

"It'll be on the other side of the road."

But it isn't. On the other side there is two, two-A and then six. Maybe there isn't a four at all. Maybe Marijke got it wrong – or Rose wrote down the number wrong.

"There's *got* to be a four."

But there isn't. We go up the street, then down the other side. Still no four. And then the door of two-A flies open and a fat woman in an apron leans out and asks, "What you looking for?"

"We can't find number four."

The woman's face creases into a smile.

"He's got you beat, has he? I tell you where he's to. He's round the corner, look, you go up to your left and there's a passage. You wouldn't believe the number we get traipsing up and down along here, looking for him."

We can still feel the woman's smile as we go round the corner. However, we would certainly never have found number four without her. There is no number and the door is round a twisty passage and then hidden by a slate porch.

"This has got to be it."

Rose lifts the big knocker in the shape of a dolphin, and bangs it down. We listen, but there is no sound of movement inside the cottage.

"She's probably still asleep."

"Try again."

And this time a voice calls sleepily from upstairs. "One minute!" and then we hear feet thumping down the same kind of narrow, creaky cottage stairs that I have at home. The door opens.

It must be Marijke. Her hair is sticking up all round her head in a pale yellow cloud and her face hasn't woken up yet, but she's smiling and holding the door wide.

"Rose! You came!"

We shuffle into the tiny front room, and I look around while Rose tells Marijke who I am. There is no furniture at all, just a bare room with a stone floor. Marijke catches me looking and shrugs. "It's OK for one night," she says. "I have my sleeping-bag upstairs. But there's nothing to eat here, not even a cup of coffee, so we go to a café now, and you tell me everything. And then we go to the tent." And she smiles. By now her face has woken up. In spite of the cloudy pale hair she isn't at all a fluffy person. She is very tall, and her face is strong, and determined. Marijke looks safe. Rose really will be all right with her.

"We must have a big breakfast," says Marijke as we walk towards the café. "A celebration breakfast, Rose, now you are here. And Katie will be hungry after waking so early."

Marijke speaks beautifully clear English, much clearer than mine or Rose's, although she is Dutch. I ask her how she learned and she says everyone in Holland has to learn languages, because nobody outside Holland speaks Dutch.

"So we are lucky, because Dutch is like a secret language between us."

The café has big squashy sofas, and we collapse into them while Marijke orders pancakes with strawberries, maple syrup and whipped cream, and hot chocolate. I can't wait for them to come. It seems like hours since we woke up, and we didn't dare make any breakfast at home for fear of waking Mum. The waitress brings a jug of maple syrup, a bowl of whipped cream, and then a tower of brown-and-gold pancakes, crisp at the edges and plump and sweet in the middle. But just as she sets the pancake tower down on the table, a flash of panic shoots through me. Mum! She'll be waiting. She'll think something's happened to me and she'll be so scared. I said in my note that I'd phone her from a call box –

"Is there a phone in this café?"

The waitress shakes her head.

"Oh no! Marijke, have you got a mobile I could borrow just for a minute?"

"I am sorry, Katie, I have my mobile but it is at the cottage with my sleeping bag. We could go back there for you to make your call."

"No, you're having breakfast – I'll find a call box. Rose, I've got to go. Mum'll be so scared. She won't know where I am."

"Take some pancakes, you will be hungry, Katie," says Marijke, and she wraps two pancakes in a paper napkin for me. "But your hot chocolate is coming now –"

"She's got to go," says Rose, and stands up. "Katie, I'll see you."

"Yes, see you soon, Rose –"

But I'm not really thinking properly about Rose, only about Mum and how worried she'll be, and it's all my fault. I bang my leg on the table as I try to get out. and then I drop the pancakes so that I have to scrabble to pick them up because it was so nice of Marijke to wrap them up for me. But they've got fluff on them now – yuck.

"Katie!"

It's Rose.

"Katie, I wanted to say –"

Quick, Rose, quick, just say it then I can find a call box and call Mum –

But Rose hesitates, flushing red.

"I wanted to say thank you. For coming with me."

And suddenly, surprisingly, she reaches out and gives me a hug. And I hug her back, making sure I don't cover her with pancakes and maple syrup, not wanting to rush away any more, just wanting Rose to know that I am her friend, and I do like her, and I wish there was more time.

"See you."

"See you."

"And tell Zillah –"

"Tell her what?"

"You know. Tell her to get better."

CHAPTER EIGHTEEN

Call box. I'm sure there's one up by the bank. Or maybe before that, near the post office? Why's that car hooting at me? I'm not on the road, I'm on the pavement –

"Katie! KATIE!"

And leaning out of the driver's window and waving is Mrs T.

"Katie!"

"Oh, hello Mrs T," I say, trying to make it sound as if I'm often out in Newlyn on my own first thing in the morning. Behind Mrs T a huge four-wheel drive car hoots long and loud. She's holding up the traffic.

"Idiotic man," says Mrs T fiercely, shooting the four-wheel drive a dagger look. "Where does he think he is – Hyde Park Corner? Katie, I'll pull up over there, by the parking bay. Mind you cross at the zebra crossing!"

I could escape, but I don't really want to. Mrs T is bound to find out all about me leaving Mum a note, and going off with Rose, but I don't really care any more. Mrs T is my friend. She may be a grown-up, but she's a friend first.

I cross carefully at the zebra crossing (the four-wheel drive doesn't stop for me) and open the passenger door of Mrs T's battered old Nissan, which is usually full of chickens and children.

"Jump in, Katie. Move that apple first, it's mouldy – and check the front of the seat, Josh got hold of chewing-gum yesterday. Oh, how I hate, loathe and detest this car. It's a litter bin on wheels. What's that in your hand, Katie?"

"Pancakes. But they've got carpet fluff on them."

"Chuck them on the floor. Is your mum shopping?"

"No, she's ... um, she's back at home."

"Are you here on your own?"

"Well, not, not really . . . I came with Rose."

"Rose? Oh, the girl at the campsite. I know. So where is she?"

"Um – she's having breakfast with a friend."

"Mysteriouser and mysteriouser," says Mrs T. "What sort of a friend, if you don't mind me asking?"

"She's called Marijke. She's Dutch, and she's really nice. Rose lived with her one summer. She's going to stay with her again because her mum and Jesse have gone away."

"Have they now? And Rose doesn't want to go with them?"

"No. She doesn't – I don't think she really likes Jesse. Or his brother."

Mrs T frowns, looking at her hands on the steering-wheel.

"And where do the pancakes come in?"

"Marijke wrapped them up for me. They didn't have carpet fluff on them then, it was before I dropped them."

Mrs T turns round and gives me her sudden, flashing smile. "I think I've worked out most of it," she says. "Even the pancakes are falling into place now. But what about you? Why are you here, Katie?"

"Well ... Rose was coming on her own, and I thought..." But it's going to sound so stupid. I can't tell Mrs T what I thought.

"What did you think?"

Or perhaps I can tell her.

"I thought that if something happened to Rose on the way – if she got kidnapped or had an accident or something – no one would ever know. Her mum would think she was with Marijke. Marijke would think she had decided to stay with her mum."

"Yes," says Mrs T slowly. "That's true. So you came with her. Does your mum know?"

"I left a note."

"A note! Oh, Katie. Quick, what's your phone number?"

And in less than ten seconds her mobile is out and she's dialled my number.

"Oh hello, Maggie, how are you? Yes, it is a lovely morning, isn't it?" (Mrs T turns and makes a surprised face at me. I can hear Mum's voice and it sounds perfectly normal. Not worried at all.) "Oh, I'm so sorry, did I wake you? You and Katie are having a lie-in?"

Mum must have got the phone plugged in by her bed. She hasn't seen my note. She hasn't even been downstairs yet!

"No, I just rang to say I met Katie a little while ago and

we're having a chat. I haven't seen her for ages. I'll bring her back in about half an hour. Do you want a word with her?"

And she passes the phone to me.

"Er ... hello, Mum."

"Katie, I thought you were still in bed! Did you go up for the milk? Tell Annie it was nice of her to phone, but I wasn't worried about you, I didn't even know you were out of the house."

Mum doesn't know I'm in Newlyn. She probably thinks that Mrs T drove over to our village for something and met me there. But she won't think that for long, not once she reads my note.

"I'll be back soon, Mum. Have a nice rest in bed. You must be tired."

And don't go downstairs. Don't look on the kitchen table. Don't read my note.

"Mum, I'll make you breakfast in bed when I get back."

"If that doesn't make her suspicious, nothing will," says Mrs T when I've ended the call. "You'll have to tell her."

"But if she stays in bed she won't even see my note."

"Katie. You'll still have to tell her. I can't keep secrets like that from your mum."

And I know it's true.

"You must be absolutely starving," says Mrs T. "Look in the glove compartment. There should be some M-U-N-C-H-I-E-S in there."

(Mrs T is so used to spelling out the names of sweets

in case her little kids guess what she's talking about, that she even does it when the children aren't here.)

I eat the Munchies, while Mrs T drives. I feel really tired now. Rose is in the café eating pancakes with Marijke, and I'm driving safely back with Mrs T. Everything is fine.

Except for the most important thing of all.

"How's Zillah?" asks Mrs T. "Did you speak to her yesterday?"

And I'm intending to answer the question, but different words come out instead. "I wish I could see her," I say. "I miss her so much."

Mrs T drives for a while and then says, "Zillah can't risk any infections when her immune system is so weak because of the chemo. You know that and I know it. But it's very hard."

"Janice is there all the time. And Geoff goes whenever he can."

"I know. But parents are allowed, that's the way it is."

"Zillah doesn't even want Janice there all the time."

Mrs T sighs. "Poor Janice. She is so desperately worried about Zillah. She can't bear to leave her."

"It's driving Zillah crazy."

"I'm sure it is. I'm planning to go up there at the weekend. Richard is having the children and I'm taking Janice out. We're going to have a seaweed massage, a facial and an enormous lunch. My mother sent me a hundred pounds for my birthday and I am determined that it's not going to be spent on computer software or chicken feed."

"That sounds nice," I say faintly. I cannot imagine Janice having a seaweed massage, or indeed any sort of massage at all, and I'm not entirely sure what a facial is. Nor am I sure what Janice will think of it. A good wash with antiseptic soap is Janice's idea of a beauty treatment.

"Have you told her?" I ask.

"Certainly not," says Mrs T briskly. "It's a surprise."

It will be. Imagine Janice all wrapped up in seaweed.

"Nearly there," says Mrs T. "What a beautiful morning."

The sun is dazzling, and the sea is completely calm. It's a perfect day to take *Wayfarer* out – or practise diving off the rocks – or sunbathe in the orchard –

No Zillah, and now no Rose, either. Mrs T stops the car at the top of the farm lane that runs down to our house.

"I must rush, I've left Richard with those children for two solid hours. He'll be emailing Yakutsk for support by now. Now, will you be all right, Katie?"

I nod.

"You don't look all right."

And suddenly, for the first time since I heard about Zillah, I know I'm going to cry. It is too horrible. Why Zillah? Why did it happen to her? Why should Zillah have cancer in her blood cells? Acute lymphoblastic leukaemia. Everybody calls it ALL, as if that makes it sound better, but it doesn't.

I wish we could go back to the end of term. I wish it could be Zillah and me again, Zillah throwing her book-bag over the hedge, Zillah trying to make me chuck out my headless Barbies, Zillah and me sharing out our waitress tips. If only I could shut my eyes and just go back. And then make it so that the bad things would never happen... Maybe, if you can change the future, you can also change the past ... but if you go back in time, then the past becomes the future, doesn't it? Time changes, if you are looking at it from a different place. Time makes me feel dizzy.

"Katie?"

But I can't answer.

Mrs T reaches across the passenger seat and hugs me. She smells nice, of flowers. She doesn't say anything, for which I'm grateful. I am so tired of people telling me that Zillah is a fighter and she will soon be in remission, and how everything is being done for her that can possibly be done, and how brilliant the treatment is these days, and about the percentage of children who completely recover from ALL. When people tell me these things it makes me feel as if I'm not allowed to be upset, or scared. But I am very, very scared.

"There now," says Mrs T, and she gets out a wodge of tissues and wipes my face as if I was a little kid like her Josh.

I take a deep breath. "Mrs T, do you think Zillah will die?"

Mrs T doesn't answer immediately. It is so quiet that we can hear the cows chomping their grass, on the other side of the hedge. Then she passes me her comb to comb my hair and says, "No. I don't think so. And Granny

Carne doesn't think so either."

"How do you know?"

"I went to see her."

A warm breath of relief fills me. Of course. Why didn't I think of going to see Granny Carne again? Granny Carne would know. Granny Carne must be right about Zillah. She is tall and wild like a sheltering tree that blows in a gale but never breaks or falls. She would know for sure. It is her job to know about the time to come, and what will happen in it.

"Blast! Hell! Ow! Those bloody, bloody children!"

Mrs T was right to warn me about chewing-gum. A big lump of it was hiding on the gum-coloured back of the passenger seat. It is now on my hair, and on Mrs T's hair from when she leaned over to give me a hug. Mrs T drags the comb furiously through her hair and the gum.

"Ow! I have told Joshie a million times he is not allowed to take Richard's chewing-gum, but does he listen? And why, for heaven's sake, can't he spit it out on the floor like normal people? Blast! Damn! I can't get it out. How can one little piece of chewing-gum possibly stretch so far?"

I examine the pink stringy stuff in my hair.

"I think it's bubblegum."

"Oh God, and now it's all over your hair – what will Maggie say –"

"It's OK, Mum knows how to get it out with ice cubes, she's brilliant at it. I stuck some behind my ear once when I was little and she got it all out of my hair."

She will have to be very brilliant, I think as I climb out

of the car and wave goodbye to Mrs T, who is still cursing as she crashes the car into gear and shoots off. Joshie's spat-out bubblegum is going to be a serious test of Mum's ice-cube technique. Yuck.

CHAPTER NINETEEN

August 19th

Two weeks and three days since Zillah went into hospital. Every day the sun shines. Days and days and days of summer holiday which run as slowly as the thick black treacle Janice uses to bake gingerbread.

The CREAM TEAS sign still says CLOSED. The patches of yellow grass where the van and the tent and Great-Gran's blue sofa stood are growing green again. New holiday people have come.

Mum told me I should keep busy, so I've sanded the old paint off the inside of our kitchen door, repainted the door and the window sills, and next week I'm going to paint the window frames. Mum has designed a mural which I'm painting on the side of the garden shed. It's a picture of a gate opening into a mysterious green garden. It's called a *trompe l'oeil*, Mum says, because the mural tricks your eyes into thinking that there's another, beautiful garden beyond the painted gate. So I have to work very carefully and realistically. It's almost like painting a photograph. It's difficult to get it right, but the good thing is that I forget all about time while I'm painting. All I think about are the colours, and which brush to use, and whether the paint is thick enough, and will there be enough of that deep, rich green. When Mum brings out sandwiches for lunch I'm surprised to find that half the day has gone. I'm getting like Mum – she always forgets about meals when she's working in her studio.

Every morning and evening I go up to the farm to do Janice's hens. The worst bit is making sure they are all shut up safely in the henhouse at night. They are very independent and extremely annoying as well as stupid, and they don't understand about foxes. They hide in the orchard, in the hedges, in long grass, in bushes, even in the kitchen if someone's left the door open. Luckily they are greedy as well as thick and I can usually get them in by pretending it is feeding time, and calling to them the way Janice does.

I told Geoff that Mum and me don't mind cleaning out the henhouse as long as he tells us what to do. BIG MISTAKE.

I pick Janice's raspberries for her and put them in the freezer. There's usually at least a pound, sometimes two pounds. They look like jewels when they are frozen. When Janice comes back, she'll make jam from them and next year, when things are back to normal, there will be raspberry jam for the cream teas. There are also loads of beans to pick and I top and tail them and put them in freezer bags too.

Geoff doesn't talk much. He works and works and works, and his face is creased up with tiredness and worry. I never ask him about Zillah because he hates talking about her being ill. Mum talks to Janice on the phone instead, and then she tells me what Janice says. Anyway, I'm always talking to Zill, or emailing her. But when Geoff saw the henhouse after me and Mum had finished cleaning it out, he cleared his throat and said, "Don't think I don't appreciate what you're doing, Katie. You're a good girl. It puts Janice's mind at rest to know that her hens are being well cared for."

Geoff went up to the hospital last Saturday and stayed until Sunday, but most of the time he's got to carry on with the farm work. Over the weekend people from neighbouring farms came in to do the milking and all the million other jobs you can't leave for a minute if you're a farmer.

So time is doing two things. It's moving slowly, drop by drop, and it's also rushing by because of all the busyness we pack into every day. The only time I'm not doing something is when I'm in bed, waiting to fall asleep. I try not to get started with thinking. I try to imagine my island in the middle of the deep blue sea, and the noise of the waves lapping. Sometimes it works, but mostly it doesn't.

Because all the time, in the middle of all the busyness, I'm waiting. I wake up with a tight, expectant feeling in my stomach. The only other time I've had that feeling is when we were doing SATs at school. But this is every day. Painting the mural makes it dissolve for a while, but then it comes back.

Mum and I have read loads more stuff about the type

of leukaemia Zillah's got. Mum keeps printing it off the Internet, and we've got all the leaflets the hospital gave to Janice. Some of it is quite complicated and hard to understand. Some of it I don't really want to read, but I do, because if Zillah has got to have all these tests and treatment, it is pathetic of me not even to read about them.

Mum has drawn me a map showing where Zillah is in the stages of treatment, and what will come next. She has drawn a tiny little Zillah, with a backpack, hiking on a long twisty road with signposts and detours and little roads leading off it. At the moment Zillah is climbing a steep hill labelled Remission Induction. If she gets to the top of the Remission Induction Hill, that means the chemo has destroyed nearly all her cancerous cells. But to stop them growing again, she'll carry on having treatment for two years, maybe three. But she won't be in hospital all that time. She'll be back at home, and she'll even be able to go to school.

Sometimes people don't go into remission straight away, and they have to do another course of treatment. Another huge hill. But I'm not going to think about that.

I usually email Zillah as soon as I get up, because she wakes really early in the hospital. We can't phone each other as often as we want, because it costs too much. But guess what? Mrs Pascoe at the post office has sent Zillah ten pounds in phonecards.

Dear Zill

Bad news. Susie Buryan got the Guides to pray for you round the camp-fire last night. And then they sang Kum Bi Yah (hope that is how you spell it) and Susie felt sure that God was listening. She phoned me so I could tell you. Hope you're not feeling worse as a result. Mark phoned too, he and Bryony are coming over on Bouncer. Have you managed to read the lucky bead yet?

I have cleared out the boat-shed. There were four dead crabs (I've kept one for you to see because it was the biggest we've ever had in the boat-shed), a fish skeleton (how did that get there?), loads of old rope and about half a tonne of seaweed. That reminds me, did your mum enjoy the seaweed massage? Maybe we could sell our seaweed to the massage place. Now the shed's all clean for Wayfarer in the winter.

Are you OK today?

Loads of love, Katie.

PS Is God crazy enough to listen to the Guides singing Kum Bi Yah? What do you think? If I were God in that situation, I'd pretend to be deaf.

Dear Katie

God is definitely deaf at the moment. I was sick four times in the night although I have got drugs to stop it. Amy was sick too (that's my friend here, the only other patient who isn't a little kid). Amy's got worse ALL than me. Her first remission induction didn't work so she's having more chemo. We write notes because Amy is being barrier-nursed and even her mum can't

be with her at the moment, because she's got a cold.

I think she's quite lucky. Not about the chemo, but about having a rest from her mum.

I feel strange and a bit crazy today. Sorry. Dr Prashad says chemo does your head in sometimes. I like him because he talks to me, not to Mum like some doctors. Also he does not pretend chemo is great because it's making me better.

Chemo is ——–.

You can fill in the space with the worst words you know.

Chemo is ————————————————————————————

Something so scary happened last night. I couldn't remember what Wayfarer looked like. My mind kept jiggling round but it wouldn't make the right picture. I woke up all sweaty and then I looked at your mum's drawing and I remembered everything, even what the oars feel like.

I can read the writing on the lucky bead now.

Sorry, I'm going to sleep again.

LOL Zill

Dear Zill

So sorry you are feeling bad. Mum sends her love and if there is anything else you want her to do a drawing of, just say. Everyone I see in the village asks about you.

What did the writing say? (Don't bother to answer if you are still feeling bad.)

I watched Barney the Dinosaur with the little Ts

yesterday. Josh wants to send you a BIIIIIG HUG.

Lots of love, Katie

Dear Katie

It said MADE IN CHINA.

Only joking. I KNOW I read the words but now I can't remember. It's the chemo. Dr Prashad is right. It does your head in.

Mum's stopped trying to make me play games. She just sits there. It's better. Sick again.

LOL Z

Dear Zillah

I'll keep on emailing but don't email back if it makes you tired. I talked to the nurse but she said you weren't well enough to take phone calls today. It's the chemo. I'm so sorry you were sick again. Mum sends her love again.

Lots of love, Katie

(This space is for the five days when Zillah didn't phone or email. She slept nearly all the time because she had an infection. Janice phoned twice or three times a day, and Mum shut the door and talked for ages. I was really angry because I thought she was trying to hide things from me, but afterwards she said she wasn't.

"Zillah is poorly, Katie, and Janice is worn out. She hasn't had a proper night's sleep for nearly three weeks. She just needs to talk and let it all out. But I would tell you if there was any news."

This space should be as big as a book. It felt like for ever.)

CHAPTER TWENTY

August 26th

Dear Katie

I haven't been sick since yesterday. God is not completely deaf even though Susie Buryan was trying to deafen him.

Dr Prashad says I'm doing brilliantly. He came in the middle of the night and sat on my bed and talked. Mum had fallen asleep. She is so tired and I didn't want to wake her up, but I was scared. Dr Prashad showed me photos of his baby girl. He is so nice. Amy and me think he is the best doctor. We have a points system. Dr Prashad gets ten.

Sorry, got to sleep again,

LOL Zill

Dear Zill

It was so great to hear from you. I'm going to scan in a drawing Mum did of Bobby. He didn't want to sit still for it and kept wagging his tail and coming up to lick Mum. But I think it's quite good. I explained to Bobby that the drawing was for you, and he got so excited when he heard your name that he started thumping his tail on the floor.

Mr T says I can keep the school computer until the end of the holidays, so I can keep on emailing you, and guess what? I'm getting a mobile for my birthday! Only three and a half months to wait.

But you won't still be in hospital then.

Here's the picture of Bobby:

Loads of love from Katie XXXXX

Dear Katie

I am in remission. Dr Prashad told me this morning. God has got a hearing-aid at last.

LOL Zill

CHAPTER TWENTY-ONE

September 4th

Only two days before school starts. Secondary school. I've been so scared about Zillah that there hasn't been time to be scared about starting a new school.

It won't be both of us going, not yet. Just me. Zillah will be in hospital for another two weeks. But there will be loads of other people I know. Everyone from primary will be there, which is good news in some cases and not so good in others. Please, please, Susie, don't get everyone praying for Zillah at secondary school!

School on Monday. But before that, tomorrow, it's the very first day Zillah's been allowed visitors apart from Geoff and Janice. Mum and I are driving up to Bristol this afternoon, staying in a bed and breakfast, seeing Zillah in the morning and then driving back in the afternoon. It's a hundred and eighty miles to Bristol, and Mum's van doesn't go fast.

I've got so much stuff to take for Zillah.

Drawings the little Ts have done for her, cards from Mark and Bryony and Mrs Pascoe and Mrs

Isaacs at our old school, and Jenny Pendour and loads of other people. Mr and Mrs T have bought books for Zillah, because they know she eats up books like other people eat up Mars bars. Mum's got her a sketchbook and a set of charcoal pencils. I found a beautiful carved wooden box in St Ives, for Zillah to keep the lucky bead in. When her hair grows long again, she can have the bead put into a wrap.

But the most surprising present came this morning, in a bright red packet. It was from Rose, and the packet was addressed to me. Inside there was a note, and a little parcel wrapped in tissue paper and sellotaped firmly.

Dear KAYTE

I am doing ALL RIHGT with Marijke. Lots of the HAIR-WRAPPING here in Newlen. I saw my GG and she says, GIVE THIS TO YOUR FREIND becas, hospitels are NO GOOD.

See you KAYTE

YOUR FREIND

ROSE

I pressed the parcel. It felt soft and a bit crunchy, like pine-needles. It wasn't mine to open, it was Zillah's - but I was sure it was some of Great-Gran's special tea.

• • •

September 5th

Mum has finally managed to park the van, after hours of circling round and swearing. Everything is fast and noisy here, and there are traffic wardens roaming with tickets to slap on your car, even though it's Sunday. Janice told Mum that Bristol is famous for car-clamping.

The bed-and-breakfast was miles from the hospital, and it was on a big main road. I couldn't sleep much, because of the traffic and doors banging and people shouting late at night, and a police helicopter circling overhead for hours. I'd forgotten what cities are like. When I lived in London I never noticed the noise.

Nearly there. A bright new building, shiny tiles, people rushing along corridors. Everyone seems to know where to go except me and Mum.

Mum says she does know where to go. It's along this corridor, left, and we'll find the sister's office just on our right.

I'm so scared. What if Zillah's different? What if she looks awful? What if I don't know what to say?

Mum's talking to the sister. The sister's asking questions but I don't listen. My heart is thudding so hard that I can't really notice what's happening.

"She's just down there," says Mum. "She's awake. Remember, Katie, we're only staying a short time. Down there, straight on."

"But Mum – aren't you coming?"

"No, you go first, Katie. It's you she wants to see."

• • •

There's a tall, narrow bed with someone lying on it, listening to something through headphones. The bed is like a high-tech ship heading out to sea, hung with tubes and wires. And for a second I don't recognize the person on the bed, because I'm searching for a girl with dark wild curls round her face, even though I know that person doesn't exist any more.

The girl in the blue bandanna turns to look at the door, and sees me. She takes off her headphones. Her face is pale, a bit puffy. She looks at me uncertainly.

"Katie?"

"Zillah?"

"Is it really you?"

"Of course it's me. Why? Do I look different?"

"No," says Zillah. "But these drugs make me have so many dreams. The dreams are realler than what's really happening." She digs her heels into the bedclothes and pushes herself up on the pillows.

"Come and sit on the bed."

I sit down very cautiously. I don't like the look of the machines – or those tubes snaking their way out under the bedclothes...

"You can push the drip-stand out of the way," says Zillah.

"?"

"That thing there. Just push it up towards the top of the bed a bit."

"But what if I—"

"What if you what?"

"Hurt you or something?"

"Oh Katie," says Zillah. "You're scared."

"No, I'm not."

"Yes, you are. You think I'm going to break if you touch me. You think if you do anything wrong I'll collapse and die. Don't you?"

"No, I don't!"

"It's OK, Katie. That's what I thought when I first came, too. The first time I saw Amy I wanted to run away. She looked SO AWFUL. And then I thought, that's going to be me."

"How is she?"

"She's not in remission yet." Zillah turns. "Look, she's waving to you. I told her you were coming."

I hadn't noticed the glass partition at the end of the room. There's a girl lying in bed. Only her head is raised to look at us. Her head looks large and naked on its frail neck. And Zillah's right, she is waving. Then she lies back and closes her eyes.

"Amy had a bad night," Zillah says. "But she'll be really glad she saw you. I wouldn't tell her what you looked like, and she guessed short blonde hair and grey eyes."

"Bad guess."

"Very bad guess. She thinks you're really clever, because you write such long emails."

"You don't let her read them, Zillah!"

"No. I only tell her a bit."

"Oh."

"Amy won't be out of hospital for a while yet," says Zillah. "God still needs his ears syringed as far as Amy is concerned." And she smiles angrily, but I know she's not angry with me.

In a minute I'll get out the presents, and the cards. I'll give Zillah Great-Gran's packet of special tea. I wonder if the nurses will let her drink it? Mum said it wasn't likely. In a minute we'll talk. I can see the lucky bead winking on the top of Zillah's locker. Any minute now, I feel sure, I'll be able to read what it says.

"I like your bandanna," I say.

"I had all my hair cut off. I wasn't going to wait for it to fall out. If anyone at school asks, "Did your hair fall out because you had cancer?" I'll say, "No. I just decided to cut it off."

"They won't dare ask," I say. "Not if you give them that look."

"What look?"

"The scary one."

"Got to keep in practice," says Zillah. "I'm trying to make my blood cells show some respect."

Zillah, pale and puffy with no hair, wearing a blue bandanna.

Zillah, fierce and determined, her eyes flashing with life. Zillah has never been more Zillah-ish.

"I'm glad you're here, Katie," she says.

"Me too," I say. "I mean, I'm glad you're here. But I don't mean that I'm glad you're in here –"

"I know what you mean," says Zillah.

Zillah, and me.